Dear Reader,

I just wanted to tel
my publisher has de
earlier books. Some
for a while, and am g them there are titles that
have often been requested.

I can't remember a time when I haven't written, although it was not until my daughter was born that I felt confident enough to attempt to get anything published. With my husband's encouragement, my first book was accepted, and since then there have been over 130 more.

Not that the thrill of having a book published gets any less. I still feel the same excitement when a new manuscript is accepted. But it's you, my readers, to whom I owe so much. Your support—and particularly your letters—give me so much pleasure.

I hope you enjoy this collection of some of my favourite novels.

Anne Mather

Back by Popular Demand

With a phenomenal one hundred and thirty books published by Mills & Boon, Anne Mather is one of the world's most popular romance authors. Mills & Boon are proud to bring back many of these highly sought-after novels in a special collector's edition.

ANNE MATHER: COLLECTOR'S EDITION

1 JAKE HOWARD'S WIFE
2 SCORPIONS' DANCE
3 CHARADE IN WINTER
4 A FEVER IN THE
     BLOOD
5 WILD ENCHANTRESS
6 SPIRIT OF ATLANTIS
7 LOREN'S BABY
8 DEVIL IN VELVET
9 LIVING WITH ADAM
10 SANDSTORM

11 A HAUNTING
      COMPULSION
12 IMAGES OF LOVE
13 FALLEN ANGEL
14 TRIAL OF INNOCENCE
15 THE MEDICI LOVER
16 THE JUDAS TRAP
17 PALE ORCHID
18 CAROLINE
19 THE SHROUDED WEB
20 A TRIAL MARRIAGE

THE MEDICI LOVER

BY
ANNE MATHER

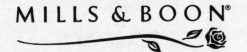

MILLS & BOON®

*MILLS & BOON and MILLS & BOON with the Rose Device
are registered trademarks of the publisher.*

*First published in Great Britain 1977 by Mills & Boon Limited
This edition 1998
Harlequin Mills & Boon Limited,
Eton House, 18-24 Paradise Road, Richmond, Surrey TW9 1SR*

© Anne Mather 1977

ISBN 0 263 80567 0

*Set in Times Roman 10 on 12 pt by
Rowland Phototypesetting Limited
Bury St Edmunds, Suffolk*

74-9804-50422

*Printed and bound in Spain
by Litografia Rosés S.A., Barcelona*

CHAPTER ONE

EVER since the sleek Trident had circled low over the lagoon before making a smooth landing at Venice's international airport, Suzanne had been concerned. No, even before that, she conceded silently to herself, watching Pietro's square hands as they lightly circled the driving wheel of his sports car. And concerned did not seem a strong enough adjective either. Disturbed, anxious—even uneasy might have described her feelings better. For as they drew nearer and nearer Pietro's home, she became more and more convinced that she should not have given in to the impulse to come.

What did she know of his family, after all? That he had no brothers or sisters, and that his father was dead. More than that he had seemed curiously loath to reveal, and had Suzanne not found the opportunity to get out of London at this time to her advantage, she would probably never even have considered his invitation.

And yet wasn't she being unnecessarily harsh with herself? After all, she and Pietro were good friends, and although she sensed that he was hoping their friendship might blossom into something more emotional, there was no reason why she should blame herself for a situation which had been of his making.

All the same, in other circumstances she would

have thought twice, and possibly three times, before committing herself to several days in the company of people she had never met, and who were not of her own nationality. Just because she could speak the language and had spent several months last year as courier for the company she worked for at their hotel in Rimini, it did not mean she understood the people.

She and Pietro Vitale had only known one another six weeks. At present, she was working in London, employed at the company's hotel in the West End, and her meeting with the young Italian had been quite coincidental. Later, he had told her he was studying at the London College of Art, but that morning, in the little antique shop in the Portobello Road, he had been just another tourist trying to make himself understood to an uncomprehending assistant. Appreciating his difficulties, Suzanne had automatically intervened, forgetting for the moment her own reasons for entering the shop. The dark-skinned Italian had not been unappreciative of the combination of thickly-lashed brown eyes and streaked honey-blonde hair that swung silkily about Suzanne's shoulders, but eventually, between them, they had made the assistant understand that he wanted to price a bronze figurine of the Virgin and Child. He wanted it as a present for his mother, he said, but it had been too expensive and he had had to decline. Afterwards, it had been natural for him to invite her to have coffee with him, and Suzanne had accepted, more out of sympathy for him than a longing to further their acquaintance. But sitting in the coffee shop only a few yards away, she had seen the sleek Mercedes, which had driven her to take refuge in the antique shop in the first place, cruising by on the opposite side of the road, and had felt more relaxed than she had done for weeks.

Pietro had proved to be an entertaining companion, and when he had suggested a second meeting, she had agreed. If her motives had more to do with the cruising Mercedes and less with a genuine desire to go out with him, she excused herself on the grounds that Pietro had invited her, and would have been disappointed if she had refused.

Even so, going back to the hotel in a cab which Pietro had hailed for her, she had had misgivings, and not until Abdul Fezik came storming into her office late that afternoon had she felt that her behaviour had been justified. Now, at least, she had a genuine reason for refusing the Turk's persistent invitations, a means to divert his attentions, with luck, towards some other member of her sex. He was a powerful and wealthy man, not used to being thwarted when it came to women, particularly not women who had to work for a living.

Suzanne, however, had had surprisingly little to do with men. From an early age, she had learned that her looks might well prove to be an obstacle in her determination to carve a career for herself. Prospective employers tended to regard attractive girls in one of two ways: either predatorily, or suspiciously; on the one hand seeking the kind of relationship Suzanne was determined to avoid, or on the other, assuming she required employment only so long as it took her to find a suitable husband. The situation infuriated Suzanne, who, having seen her own parents' marriage break up, had no intention of making the same mistakes herself.

Surprisingly though, since she came to work for the Minotaur Group three years ago, these problems had largely been avoided. Of course, that might be because she had spent so little time, comparatively speaking, in one place. During the past three years she had worked in several different countries, and at twenty-four was considered one of the company's most successful executives. Nicolai Stassis, the elderly Greek who had founded the organisation, had none of his countrymen's contempt for women, and judged his staff on their ability, not their sex. That was why she objected so strongly to Abdul Fezik's chauvinist attitude, his assumption that because she was female, she needed masculine companionship. Pietro—at that time she had not even known his surname—had seemed the answer to a prayer.

But she ought to have known that nothing was ever that simple. Pietro was not a puppet she could pull about at her own convenience, no more than Abdul Fezik could be deterred by the supposed presence of a rival. Fezik was an arrogant man, working in London for his government and living at the hotel, and Suzanne was aware that hardly anything she did went unnoticed. She sometimes wondered when he found the time to attend to his own affairs, so intent did he seem on hers. She guessed what intrigued him, of course. He was a handsome man, if a little inclined to overweight; he had money and position, almost everything a girl in her position might wish for. He couldn't accept that she did not find him as attractive as he seemed to find himself.

Her relationship with Pietro, however, was not totally one-sided. As she got to know him better, she began to enjoy his undemanding company, his gentleness, his courtesy, his sense of humour. His interest in art stemmed, he told her, from a love of beautiful things, and although he told her little about his home life, she gathered that he knew quite a lot about his own country's heritage. He was obviously not a wealthy man—his clothes were always clean and serviceable, but they were worn in places, the elbows of his jackets patched with leather. And yet, he had a certain air about him at times which was strangely out of keeping with his appearance, and Suzanne had to curb her desire to question him about his background. It was nothing to do with her, she had told herself on these occasions. No matter how likeable Pietro was, he aroused little but her affection, and a curious sense of compassion for his diffidence.

When he told her he was going home to Italy for ten days at Easter, Suzanne had not immediately considered what his absence might mean to her. In the few weeks they had known one another he had heard about her parents' divorce and her father's subsequent death in a motor accident. Her mother had married again, but it was not a happy liaison either, and Suzanne's contact with the woman who had borne her was limited to occasional lunches when her mother came up from Bristol for a day's shopping. Since Suzanne's work often kept her out of the

country for months at a time, she could not blame
her mother for their estrangement, and nowadays
they seemed to have little to say to one another.
Annabel moved in a different world from that of her
daughter, and had never desired independence as her
daughter did.

Nevertheless, when Pietro suggested that Suzanne
should come home with him for the holiday, the idea
of a family occasion had had some appeal. Granted
his family was not her family, but if his mother was
anything like Pietro himself then she would no doubt
be a charming lady. And she was free for the weekend at least. . .

Even so, she had demurred, insisting that she could
not accept such an invitation after such a brief
acquaintance. Pietro had protested that he could write
to his mother and have her invite Suzanne personally,
but still she had refused. Apart from anything else,
she was not the sort of girl to agree to spend ten
days with a young man she knew practically nothing
about, however ingenuous he might seem.

But again fate had taken a hand in the person of
Abdul Fezik. Three days after Pietro's invitation, the
hotel manager sent for Suzanne. He had a request to
make of her, he had said, half reluctantly she had
felt, immediately apprehensive. He had been
approached, he went on, by one of their guests, Mr
Fezik, who intended holding a reception in the hotel
during the Bank Holiday weekend. Mr Fezik needed
someone to act as his hostess at the reception, and
had suggested that perhaps Suzanne might be per-
suaded to accept.

Once again, Suzanne had been staggered by the man's audacity. After everything that had gone before he still would not believe that sooner or later she would not succumb to his personality. Before she knew what she was saying, she had informed the manager that regretfully she could not accept Mr Fezik's invitation, that she had already made arrangements for the weekend, that she was spending Easter in Italy with her boy-friend's family.

Surprisingly, the manager had seemed slightly relieved. Perhaps, contrary to Suzanne's beliefs, he had been aware of what was going on. In any event, he accepted her apologies with a smile, and assured her that she had no need to consider altering her arrangements.

Pietro had naturally been delighted when she had told him she had changed her mind about coming to Italy, but affronted when she suggested it might be better if she stayed at an hotel.

'Castelfalcone is just a village,' he had protested, in his heavily accented English. 'There is no hotel— just the *pensione*. It would not be right for a guest of my family to stay at the *pensione*.'

And so Suzanne had acquiesced. It was only a few days, after all. She had to return to London the following Tuesday. As they were flying out on Thursday, it was only a matter of four days.

Nevertheless, as the aircraft carrying them to Venice took off from London's Heathrow Airport, the ambiguity of her position began to make Suzanne uneasy. Pietro had told her that he had written to his mother, but not what he had said, and she couldn't help wondering whether he had implied a relationship between them that stemmed more from his imagination that reality. What if his mother questioned their association, what could she say? What would Pietro say?

Pietro's small sports car had been waiting for him at the airport. They had cleared passport control and Customs with the minimum amount of fuss, and emerged into the mild afternoon air, feeling the weight of their heavy clothes. The sky was vaguely overcast, but the light was brilliant, making Suzanne grope for her dark glasses in her bulky handbag.

Watching the other passengers making for the motorboats and buses made Suzanne wish they were staying in Venice. How much simpler it would have been to book in anonymously at some hotel, without the daunting prospect of facing Pietro's unknown relatives.

They drove north, leaving the canals and campaniles of the city behind. The autostrada was busy with holiday traffic, and Suzanne, who had never driven with Pietro before, was alarmed by his reckless disregard for other motorists. He was obviously one of those men who assumed a different character behind the wheel, and her palms were moist and she was re-assessing her opinion of him when they turned off the autostrada on to a narrower, rougher road.

In an effort to divert him and herself, Suzanne allowed herself the privilege of asking questions she had hitherto avoided. 'Do you and your mother live alone?' she queried tentatively, speaking in Italian to make it easier for him.

Pietro took a few moments before replying, pretending to concentrate on passing a farm cart drawn by a pair of rather tired-looking oxen, but eventually he said: 'No. We live in the house of my cousin.'

'Your cousin?' Suzanne's dark eyebrows arched.

Pietro nodded, his hands tightening on the steering wheel. 'I told you, Suzanne—my father died some years ago.'

'Well, yes. . .' Suzanne considered the situation. 'And your cousin lives at Castelfalcone.'

'That is correct.'

Suzanne drew her lower lip between her teeth, wishing he would be a little more forthcoming. 'Your—er—cousin is married?' she probed, and Pietro nodded once more.

Suzanne tried to picture the household. She knew Italians held very strongly to the family ideal, but two women running a home was seldom successful. What was Pietro's mother's position in the household? Were there children? Was she her nephew's housekeeper, or nursemaid to his children? Did other members of the Vitale family live in the house? Suzanne wished she had asked some of these questions before leaving London.

'What—what does your cousin do?' she queried unwillingly, and was surprised at the look of bitterness which crossed Pietro's face.

'Do?' he echoed. 'What do you mean—what does he do?'

Suzanne, who had thought the question quite a simple one, shook her head. 'I meant—what is his occupation?' she explained swiftly. 'I presume he does have one, doesn't he?'

Pietro glanced sideways at her. 'My cousin is disabled,' he stated harshly. 'He had an accident three years ago.'

'Oh!' Suzanne wished she had never asked the question. She felt as if she had intruded into some personal tragedy, although there was curiously little sympathy in Pietro's voice. 'I'm sorry.'

Pietro shrugged. 'These things happen. Mazzaro is lucky to be alive.'

'Mazzaro? That's your cousin's name?'

'Mazzaro di Falcone, yes.'

'*Falcone*?' Suzanne couldn't prevent the ejaculation. 'But. . .' She paused. 'I assumed his name would be the same as yours.'

'No.' Pietro shook his head. 'Mazzaro's father was my mother's brother.'

'I see.'

Suzanne stared out at the countryside through which they were passing. A fugitive gleam of sunlight was gilding the spire of a church she could see high up on the hillside. They were in rugged country, presently following a route that traced the winding course of a stream before rising to overlook the valley, rich with fields of ripening grain. They had passed through several villages, hamlets mostly, and ahead of them were rising the ascending plateaux of the Alps, snow-capped and magnificent, their pine-clad slopes the home of marmot and wild deer.

It was beautiful country, but Suzanne was paying little attention to the scenery. Something about

Pietro's cousin's name was familiar, and it took her several minutes to realise it was the same as the village. Or almost. Castelfalcone. . . Falcone.

'Pietro—' she began, only to have him interrupt her by asking whether she was hungry or tired, explaining that it was not much further now. His smile attempted to reassure her, and Suzanne shrugged, defeated. She would, without doubt, learn soon enough why Pietro should choose to be so reticent about his family.

Castelfalcone reminded Suzanne a little of San Marino. Like the tiny republic perched high on its mountain, Castelfalcone was a fortified community, surrounded by crenellated walls and towers, with an encircling moat of water. It was entered by one of two arched gateways, its narrow streets and arcades redolent with history. A cobbled square, the Piazza della Cortina, Pietro told her it was called, seemed the focal point of the village, and there were plenty of people still about, enjoying the cool evening air. The doors of a *trattoria* stood wide and outside people were sitting at tables which in the heat of the day could be shaded by their striped umbrellas. Trees framed the *piazza*, some already dripping with blossom.

'It's beautiful!'

Suzanne spoke involuntarily, and Pietro looked pleased. 'Yes, it is,' he agreed, casting a smiling glance in her direction. 'We get many tourists in the season.'

Suzanne glanced round as they circled the square and entered a narrow thoroughfare leading up out of the village. 'Where does your cousin live?' she asked frowning, and silently, Pietro gestured to a sign set at the side of the road just ahead of them. It read simply: '*Villa Falcone*' with an arrow directing the motorist up a steep incline. Suzanne looked up, but all she could see was stone walls from this angle, and unknowingly she held her breath as Pietro swung across the road and accelerated swiftly up the tree-lined approach to tall iron gates.

She could see the villa through the gates as Pietro went to open them, and her breathing quickened uncontrollably. She did not need to see the family crest decorating the twenty-feet-high gates to know that somehow she had got herself invited to one of Italy's stately homes, although in her experience wealthy men did not advertise themselves as that sign appeared to do down below them.

Pietro returned and got into the car, and she turned to him half impatiently. 'Why didn't you tell me?' she exclaimed, but he was putting the car into gear and would not look at her.

'Would you have come if I had?' he countered.

'Probably not.'

'That's what I thought.'

'But, Pietro, can't you see? I can't stay here!'

'Why not?' He had halted the car inside the gates and was waiting to get out to close them.

'You know why not. Pietro, if this is your cousin's home—' She sighed. 'Surely you understand.'

He looked at her then. 'Suzanne, do not concern yourself. My cousin does not have a lot of money, if that is what is worrying you.'

'He must have!'

'No.' Pietro shook his head. 'Suzanne, do you think your country is the only country to suffer from inflation and taxation? We have suffered, too. We are still suffering. There are few Italians with money today.'

'But—this place. . .'

Pietro shrugged. 'What you are looking at, Suzanne, is a—museum, no? Rooms full of furniture and paintings, cases of china and glass, goblets and medallions, shelves of books which will never be read. A mausoleum would have more life! And in a few weeks tourists will come. They will be conducted around the Villa Falcone by my mother. They will buy a guide book, and we hope a souvenir to remind them of their visit. Now do you understand?'

Suzanne understood what he was saying, but not the tone in which he was saying it. The contempt in Pietro's voice was something she had not heard before.

'But—but surely the paintings you mentioned—and other things—they must be valuable?'

'No doubt.'

'Then why doesn't—I mean, I know there's a great demand for such things today.'

Pietro stared ludicrously at her, affecting horror at her words. 'Suzanne! What you are suggesting is—blasphemous! Outrageous! *Sacrilegious!*'

The mockery in his voice made her draw in her lips. 'I gather your cousin does not want to sell,' she said flatly.

'You gather correctly.' Pietro vaulted out of the car. 'Excuse me.'

When he came back after closing the tall gates, the mockery had disappeared. Instead, he apologised as he got into the car, giving her a rather shamefaced smile.

'I am afraid I allow my cousin's selfishness to upset me at times,' he said. 'Forgive me. I am not normally so impolite.' He sighed. 'No doubt, you are wondering where we live. Well, we occupy the west wing at the back of the villa. You will see it is built on three sides of enclosed square, with a loggia where one can sit on hot days. There is a fountain in the square, and the sound of running water is delightful. I am sure you will like it.'

Suzanne wished she felt as confident. The long, south-facing portico of the villa was magnificent, of course. No one could fail to admire its classical lines, the stone façade inlaid with variegated marble, creating a pattern of light and dark over the entire building. But staying in such a place was something else. And if Pietro disliked his cousin so much, why did he stay?

They drove beneath an archway, overhung with vines, and along a tree-shaded avenue at the side of the villa, until Pietro drew up in a stone-flagged courtyard, flanked by garages and stables and various other outbuildings. An elderly man emerged from one of the buildings at their approach, but his greeting was barely civil when he recognised the car. Considering Pietro had been away for several weeks at least, Suzanne thought his welcome was less than enthusiastic. But Pietro seemed not to notice, hoisting their suitcases out of the back of the car, and bidding Suzanne to follow him.

A belt of trees shielded the villa from the stables, but the pergola-shaded walk back to the house was charming. Already Suzanne could see lights from the villa as darkness deepened amongst the trees, and a ripple of anticipation quickened her blood. Unwillingly, she was becoming intrigued by the situation here, curious to know more about the family who accepted all this magnificence as commonplace.

They came to the villa through formal gardens of lawns and hedges laid out with geometric attention to detail, and Suzanne saw the shadowy courtyard, mosaic-tiled, where a marble basin echoed to the waters of the fountain. The fluted columns of the loggia were indistinct in the fading light, but the balcony above would give a wonderful view of the surrounding countryside.

They entered into a long gallery, illuminated by wall lamps, intricately carved in bronze. All the downstairs apartments of the villa opened on to the loggia, Pietro had explained, but now the shutters were drawn against the invasion of night insects.

Their feet echoed on marble tiles, their presence seemed an intrusion to pilastered walls, decorated with panels painted in colours which had faded only slightly with the years. Suzanne looked about her in wonder—at the panelling of the arched ceiling above their heads, at a side table inlaid with ivory, at the fine-grained marble beneath their feet. There was a silver salver standing on the table, and the richness of its scrollwork put its value far beyond the reach of any ordinary individual.

Pietro put down their cases and regarded her tolerantly. 'I can see that you appreciate art and architecture, too,' he commented dryly. 'Come. We must let my—family—know we are here.'

His deliberate hesitation did not go unnoticed, and Suzanne looked down doubtfully at the purple corduroy slacks suit she was wearing. In these surroundings, trousers on a woman seemed an insult somehow. She wished she had worn a skirt. But then she had not known that Pietro's family lived in one of Italy's famous villas.

Before they could move, however, a door to their left opened, and the tall, slightly stooped figure of a man emerged. Suzanne stiffened, guessing this must be her host, but even so she was not prepared for her first meeting with the master of the Villa Falcone.

Amazingly, what struck her first about him was his eyes. Amazing, because in spite of his distorted body, she looked first into clear green eyes, deep set and thickly lashed, hooded by heavy lids. His eyes were beautiful, which made what came after much harder to look upon.

She had been expecting a younger man, for one thing. Pietro was, after all, in his early twenties, and as this man was his cousin, she had expected someone of a similar age. But Mazzaro di Falcone was much older, in his late thirties at least, and the thick black hair which fell below the level of his collar was streaked with grey in places. He was taller than the average Italian, with a lean muscular body, but he leaned heavily on two sticks, and when he moved his gait was slow and awkward, twisting his spine and obviously causing him some pain, judging by the tightness of his dark features. But it was the scarring of his face and neck which distorted his expression, giving him a vaguely malevolent appearance. He reminded Suzanne of Dante's *Fallen Angel*, and the awareness of the feelings he was arousing inside her made her uneasy.

Pietro, perhaps sensing the tension in the air, moved towards his cousin. 'Good evening, Mazzaro,' he said, gesturing to Suzanne to come forward. 'As you can see, we have arrived. Allow me to introduce you to my—to Suzanne, Suzanne Hunt.' He paused, as his cousin's eyebrows arched. 'Suzanne, as you've probably guessed, this is my cousin Mazzaro, Count di Falcone.'

'*Count*?' The word was out before Suzanne could prevent it, and the fingertips of one hand sought her lips as if in admonishment.

Mazzaro di Falcone's eyes narrowed. 'No doubt my cousin omitted to mention what is, after all, purely a nominal title, Miss Hunt,' he commented, in perfect English. 'How do you do? As you can see, I am not in a position to shake your hand, but you are welcome to the Villa Falcone.'

'Thank you.' Suzanne glanced awkwardly at Pietro. 'I—it was kind of you to permit me to come.'

Mazzaro made a dismissing gesture with his shoulders. 'Your mother is in the small salon, Pietro. I know she is awaiting your arrival with much—excitement. If you and Miss Hunt will excuse me. . .'

Again he spoke in English, but Pietro broke in quickly in his own language, almost defiantly, Suzanne felt. 'Suzanne speaks Italian fluently, Mazzaro. You don't have to demonstrate your command of English on her.'

His words were ill-chosen, almost insolent in intonation, but Mazzaro di Falcone merely regarded his cousin with slightly amused eyes. 'I gather you do not feel the need to do so,' he remarked in Italian, and Pietro's expression darkened angrily.

But Mazzaro did not wait to continue the altercation. With a faint bow of his head in Suzanne's direction, he moved away along the hall, his shadow cast upon the panelling like some grotesque caricature of a man. Pietro, too, watched his cousin's progress, and a little of the angry frustration left his face. Then he turned and took Suzanne's arm.

'Come! The small salon is this way.'

As they passed the room from which Mazzaro di Falcone had emerged, Suzanne glimpsed a high-ceilinged apartment, comfortably if sparsely furnished, with a wall of leatherbound books facing the door. But Pietro had already stopped outside an adjoining apartment, and as he pushed open double doors with a flourish, a young girl of perhaps ten years came rushing to greet him.

'Pietro! Pietro!' she cried excitedly, wrapping her arms around his middle, looking up into his face with wide-eyed delight. 'I thought you were never coming!'

Pietro bestowed a kiss on both the child's cheeks, and then looked over her head at the elderly woman seated in an armchair by the screened marble fire-place. 'Mamma!' he spoke with the warmth to which Suzanne was accustomed. 'Mamma, it is so good to see you again.'

As Pietro went to receive his mother's greeting, the child turned her attention to Suzanne, her brow furrowing with undisguised curiosity. She was a plain child, with the sallow complexion sometimes found in hotter climes, her straight black hair drawn unbecomingly back from her face in two stiff braids. And yet, when she had been greeting Pietro, animation had added warmth to her features, and it was then that Suzanne had guessed that she must be Mazzaro di Falcone's daughter. Yet she had a neglected air, as if no one really took a great deal of interest in her, and certainly her clothes did not do justice to her slim little body.

Deciding that it might be easier if she spoke first, Suzanne forced herself to smile and say: 'Hello. My name is Suzanne. What's yours?'

Before the child could reply however, Signora Vitale's voice rang out distinctly across the wide room: 'Elena! Come here. At once.'

There was something about the Italian word *avanti* which gave it a much terser sound than its English translation: 'Come'. Elena obviously responded to it, and without more ado, skipped obediently across to where Pietro's mother was sitting, leaving the outsider feeling very much alone in the doorway.

This was the small salon, thought Suzanne in wonder, realising it was almost as big as the reception area of the hotel back in England. As in the hall, the walls here were inlaid with frescoed panels, depicting hunting scenes, the realism of a stag at bay reassuring her. She felt very much like that cornered animal at this moment. Signora Vitale was very much the mistress of the situation, seated in her tapestry-covered chair, Pietro slightly behind her, Elena standing in the circle of her arm, at home with the fine grain of polished wood and the richly woven carpets.

Pietro was looking at Suzanne, too, but with a gentler appraisal, and presently he beckoned her forward and introduced her to his mother. Like Pietro's cousin, Signora Vitale was older than Suzanne had imagined, and she must have given up all hope of bearing a child before Pietro was conceived.

After greeting her son's guest with a scarcely-concealed disapproval, which Suzanne put down to the informality of her appearance, the woman asked several personal questions about her background. Although Suzanne resented this inquisition, nevertheless, she gave in to it, deciding that as she had nothing to hide, there was no reason why she should not satisfy Signora Vitale's curiosity. However, the old lady's disapproval deepened when she heard that Suzanne's parents were divorced, and in quelling tones she told the girl that there was no divorce in the eyes of God.

Pietro's expression was apologetic, and his eyes begged her not to take what his mother said too seriously. Suzanne bit her tongue on the retort which sprang to her lips, and instead spoke again to the child.

'Elena,' she said, retrieving her smile, which had become strained and had finally disappeared in the face of Signora Vitale's catechism. 'What a pretty name!'

The little girl looked up at her doubtfully. No doubt Suzanne's ability to address her in her own language had impressed her, but she still looked to Pietro's mother for guidance. That lady drew the child to her, bestowed a kiss on both cheeks and then said: 'You may go to bed now, Elena. You will have plenty of time to speak with Pietro tomorrow.'

Elena's lips drooped, but there was no trace of rebellion in the way she obediently turned to Pietro for his kiss, and then with a bob which could have been directed at both Suzanne and Signora Vitale, she went quickly out of the room, closing the doors behind her.

Suzanne was sorry to see her go. While the child had been there, the situation had held promise, at least. Now, she felt chilled and ill at ease again.

'Pietro tells me you work in an hotel, *signorina*,' the old lady continued, apparently in no way diverted by Elena's departure.

'That's right,' Suzanne nodded, smoothing her palms down over the seat of her pants. 'As a matter of fact, I worked in Rimini for several months last year.'

'Rimini!' The way the old lady's lips curled showed her opinion of Rimini. 'That tourist paradise! Is that all your experience of Italy?'

'No. No. I've visited Rome and Venice, and of

course while I was working in Rimini, I went to
Florence several times.'

'And which city did you prefer, *signorina*?'

Suzanne had the feeling it was a loaded question.
How she answered this might influence her future
relationship with Pietro's mother. Then she scoffed
at herself. What future relationship? A weekend!
Four days to justify herself.

But she could only be honest, after all. 'Florence,'
she answered without hesitation. '*La città delle
fiore*!'

Signora Vitale's expression actually softened
slightly. 'You do? You like Florence?' Her lips
twitched, and Suzanne breathed more freely. She had
obviously chosen well. 'Yes, *signorina*. Florence is
my favourite, too. The cradle of the Renaissance,
no? The pawn of the Medicis. And yet ultimately
the city triumphs over all. Immortal. Brunnelleschi,
Giotto, Pisano, Botticelli—ah, there is no end to its
treasures. How could anyone tire of its magnificence?'

Pietro was looking pleased now. 'My mother is
an expert on Renaissance art and architecture,' he
told Suzanne proudly.

'Then you must appreciate this villa,' she ventured
softly, but Signora Vitale made an impatient gesture.

'I love the Villa Falcone!' she said, with asperity.
'But not opening its rooms to unfeeling tourists who
come to poke and pry and stare and finger—'

'Zia Tommasa!' A light voice interrupted the old
lady's tirade. 'I am sure Miss Hunt would not agree
with you, would you, Miss Hunt?'

Suzanne swung round to confront a young woman standing just inside the doors of the salon. From the top of her sleekly groomed head to the Gucci shoes on her slender feet she breathed style and elegance, the swinging skirt of her printed silk dress proclaiming its exclusiveness by its very simplicity. A second appraisal, however, revealed a featherlight tracing of lines fanning out from the corners of her eyes and mouth, and Suzanne guessed she was older than she at first appeared.

'Sophia!' Pietro left his mother to approach the other woman, and she wrapped her arms around his neck and returned his impulsive embrace with an abandon which might have shocked Suzanne had she and Pietro been emotionally involved with one another.

'Pietro darling,' the woman called Sophia protested at last, drawing back from him and casting a smoothing hand over the cap of auburn-tinted hair that framed her small features appealingly. 'It's wonderful to have you home again.' Then her eyes moved to Suzanne. 'And this is your English girlfriend.' She smiled, the first really friendly smile Suzanne had received since entering the Villa Falcone. 'Welcome to Castelfalcone, Miss Hunt. We want you to enjoy your stay with us.'

'Which she won't do if you have anything to do with it, eh, Sophia?'

A shadow had fallen across them, and turning to the sound of that lazily mocking voice, Suzanne saw that Mazzaro di Falcone had come to stand in the open doorway.

At once, Pietro started forward, words of repudiation spilling from his lips, but Sophia held him back with an imperious gesture of her hand, the jewels on her fingers reflecting light in a thousand different prisms.

'You will have your little joke, won't you, Mazzaro?' she said teasingly, speaking in English as he had done, making light of something which for a moment had been anything but. 'Miss Hunt, have you met my husband—Count di Falcone?'

'We've met,' retorted Mazzaro coolly, his curiously green eyes flickering over Suzanne's flushed face before shifting to Signora Vitale. 'Dinner is waiting, Zia Tommasa, and Lucia insists that she will not be held responsible if it spoils.'

CHAPTER TWO

SUZANNA'S fingers trembled as she silently released the catch on the balcony door. The last thing she wanted to do was to arouse anyone else to the awareness that she could not sleep, but she had lain sleepless for hours now and she needed some air.

The door swung open on oiled hinges, and she breathed a sigh of relief. The cool air was chilling, but refreshing, and her heated body responded eagerly. Closing her eyes for a moment, she lifted a hand to brush her hair back from her face. Oh, that was good, after the tormenting confusion of troubled impressions stirring her into consciousness.

She glanced back at the shadowy room behind her. Certainly the room was comfortable enough, and the bed quite luxuriously soft, but still she was restless. There were too many things to keep her awake, and not even the exhaustion of the journey was sufficient to banish the memories of the evening she had just spent.

She stepped out on to the balcony and moved to the rail, looking down on to the courtyard below. Even the fountain was silent now and only the breeze blowing down from the mountains made music through the columns of the loggia. She shivered. The negligee she had pulled on over her chiffon nightgown was scarcely a barrier to temperatures dipping in the hours before dawn, but still she lingered, loath to return to the turmoil she had found on her pillow. Somehow she had to come to terms with the situation here, but it wasn't going to be easy.

Her eyes lifted to the mountains, their bulk a rugged landmass on the skyline. How could anyone live in such surroundings without being affected by a feeling of immortality? she wondered. But did that give one the right to treat someone else with contempt? Her brows drew together in a troubled frown. There were four adults and one child living at the villa, and between them they represented the whole gamut of human relationships. No wonder Pietro had been loath to discuss his family. How could anyone accurately describe the situation at the Villa Falcone?

Yet there seemed no reason for the tension she could feel just below that surface veneer of civility. Pietro's mother was not the easiest person to get along with, she conceded, but she was old, and that excused a lot. Pietro's attitude was a little less easy to understand. He obviously loved his mother and Elena, and he appeared to hold a great affection for Sophia. But he and his cousin seemed totally opposed to one another. Sophia, on the face of it, had the rawest deal. She seemed a perfectly normal friendly young woman, interested in Suzanne's work, in her life in England and the places she had visited. She discussed the advantages of working in different countries with real enthusiasm, and was the only person at the dinner table to make Suzanne feel at ease. But it was her husband who acted as a catalyst on all of them, and Suzanne shivered again as she recalled her own disturbing reactions to Mazzaro di Falcone.

Dressed in black, which accentuated his brooding malevolence, he sat at the head of the long, polished dining table with the cool despotism of a Medici. The magnificent room matched his mood for period. Subdued lights, and scented candles burning in a bronze holder, cast shadows up to the carved ceiling, disguising the ugly weals that began below the Count di Falcone's right eye, spreading across his cheek and running down the side of his neck. The collar of his silk shirt was open, and Suzanne had had to force herself not to stare at the spot where the scars disappeared beneath the fine material.

But it was not just his appearance that disturbed her. His scarred face did not repel her, rather the reverse, and she was made increasingly conscious of the penetration of green eyes when she gave in to the temptation to look at him. It was his behaviour towards his wife, however, which seemed so illogical, that aroused the most distracting emotions inside her. And it was this, more than anything, that she found hardest to assimilate.

Throughout the meal, Sophia had made repeated attempts to draw her husband into the conversation, and on each occasion he had repulsed her efforts with some mocking or scathing retort. He seemed to take pleasure in being rude to her, but she merely dismissed his insolence with a reluctant smile, continuing to talk to Suzanne as if nothing untoward had happened. But Suzanne knew it had happened, and so did Pietro, sitting across from her, judging by the way his hands were clenched where they rested on the table.

It was obvious that Pietro resented his cousin's behaviour towards his wife. And why not? It was a perfectly natural reaction. And yet the courtesy which Mazzaro showed to his aunt negated his dismissal as a boor. So why did he treat Sophia in that way? And why didn't she retaliate? If he spoke to her like that, Suzanne knew she would. But in Sophia di Falcone's position, would she want to. . .?

She looked down at her fingers gripping the wrought iron, and as she did so a shadow moved in the courtyard below. She started violently, stepping back from the rail, her mouth suddenly dry. Someone was down there. But who? And why? And had they seen her?

Even as she stood, transfixed, the shadow moved again and materialised into the tall, lean figure of a man, a man who moved stiffly, as if unused to such movements.

Suzanne pressed her hand to her lips to prevent the involuntary ejaculation that hovered there. It was Mazzaro di Falcone. She could see him now, the darkness of his head, the muscular width of his body. But Mazzaro di Falcone walking *without* his sticks, unevenly to be sure, limping a little, but definitely upright.

For a few moments longer she stood motionless, and then realising she ought not to be seeing this, she stepped silently back towards her balcony door. It didn't make sense. Mazzaro walking the courtyard in the early hours of the morning—walking alone

and unaided. Did anyone know? Had he confided in
anybody? Or was this his secret, the reason he treated
his wife with such contempt? Obviously, Sophia
could not know about this, or she might be a little
less patient with him. But what possible motive could
he have for keeping it a secret, for denying his family
the joy of knowing he was getting so much better?

Shedding her negligée, Suzanne tumbled back into
bed, feeling more confused now than she had done
before. And yet, for all that, she fell asleep almost
immediately.

She awakened to the sound of someone knocking at
her door. For a moment, it was difficult to get her
bearings, but the sunlight shafting through the still-
open door to the balcony brought awareness into
sharp perspective. Struggling up against the cream
silk-cased pillows, she called: '*Avanti*!' and the
elderly housekeeper, Lucia, came into the room
carrying a silver tray. For all the brilliant sunshine
outside, Lucia clung to dark clothes and voluminous
skirts which almost touched her ankles, but her lined
face was not unfriendly.

'*Buon giorno, signorina*,' she greeted the girl
politely, as she approached the bed across the rug-
strewn tiled floor.

'*Buon giorno*, Lucia. *Che ora sono*?'

Lucia looked pleased that Suzanne could understand her own language. '*Sono le dieci e mezzo,
signorina*,' she told her smilingly, setting the tray
across her knees. '*Ha dormito bene*?'

But Suzanne was scarcely listening to her now.

Was it really half past ten? Had she slept so long? Perhaps it was not so surprising, though, considering her disturbed night and the hour at which she finally fell asleep.

Still conversing in Italian, she said: 'There was no need for you to go to all this trouble, Lucia. I'm afraid I've overslept.'

Lucia folded her hands across her white apron. 'It is no trouble, *signorina*. And Pietro, he tells me you will be very tired.'

Suzanne examined the contents of the tray, the silver coffee service, the jug of freshly-squeezed orange juice, the chafing-dish containing hot croissants, and curls of butter in an ice-chilled bowl. Lying beside her plate was a single rose, an exquisite bloom, magnolia white, but veined with a delicate thread of palest pink.

She lifted it carefully, cradling it between her palms, inhaling its perfume. It was as delicate as it colour, and hauntingly fragnant. It was charming of Pietro to think of such a thing, but she hoped he was not reading more into her acceptance of his invitation than was really there.

'It's beautiful,' she said. 'Thank him for me, will you?'

'The Conte sent you the rose, *signorina*,' Lucia stated expressionlessly. 'They are cultivated here— at the Villa Falcone.'

Suzanne dropped the bloom as if its thorns had suddenly pierced her skin. Mazzaro di Falcone had no right to send her roses, and she felt angry with him for placing her in such an ambiguous position.

Unless. . . Unless, he had seen her in those hours before dawn, and this was his way of letting her know it. . .

'Well—thank you, Lucia,' she said now, pouring herself some orange juice with a slightly unsteady hand. 'And—and if you do see Pietro, will you tell him I shan't be long?'

Lucia moved towards the door. 'Do not alarm yourself, *signorina*. Pietro has driven his mother to the village. The Mass will not be over for some time yet.'

Of course. Suzanne felt a pang of regret. It was Good Friday. If she had not overslept, she could have gone with them.

'Has—did the—I mean, where is the Signora Sophia?' she asked, her fingers melting the frosting on her glass.

Lucia made an eloquent movement of her shoulders. 'The Contessa seldom rises before noon, *piccola*. Relax. This is a holiday for you, *no*?' She smiled. 'Until later, *signorina*,' and the door clicked shut behind her.

Suzanne finished the orange juice in her glass, and poured herself some of the strongly flavoured coffee. She drank it black with two spoons of sugar, and as she did so, she studied the rose again. It was certainly the most perfect specimen she had ever seen, just coming to fullness, its petals thick and velvety soft. But why had he sent it? she asked herself, chafing at the way her heart thumped when she thought of Mazzaro di Falcone.

Thrusting the tray aside, she swung her legs out

of bed and padded across to the long windows. She paused at the balcony doors, loath to emerge for fear of being seen in the filmy transparency of her nightgown. Had it been a dream, what she had seen last night? Had she really seen Mazzaro walking without sticks? Or had it all been wishful thinking on her part?

In spite of the turmoil of her thoughts, nothing could spoil her delight in the view that confronted her. Stretching above the walls of the villa, the hill-side was thick with larch and pine trees, a cloak of foliage reaching towards the snow-capped peaks beyond. Nearer at hand, she could see a waterfall cascading over an outcrop of rock to reappear as a stream further down the valley, and meadows bright with the yellow heads of dandelions.

But it was the villa itself which really enchanted her, its stone walls honey-tinged in the sunlight. She could hear the fountain playing and longed to dip her fingers in its depths, its coolness like a trail of ice across her skin. She raised her shoulders in a gesture of supplication, encompassing the whole beauty of her surroundings. Then she turned deter-minedly back to the room.

It was a relatively plain apartment, but as with the other rooms of the villa, the pattern of architecture was repeated. The bed was comparatively modern, although its head-board was intricately carved, and the silk sheets disguised a mattress which owed its comfort to modern technology. There were tall arched doors leading into an adjoining bathroom, which had to have been a new innovation, but the

green-veined marble tiles blended into their surroundings.

Suzanne took a shower in the sunken bath, deliberately cooling the water so that her skin tingled
pleasurably and then she tackled the contents of her
suitcases. The night before she had done little more
than drape the crushable items over the back of a
chair, and take out her nightgown and toiletries. Now
she hung her clothes away in the capacious depths
of a massively carved cabinet with a long oval mirror
giving her back her reflection.

It was difficult deciding what to wear. In the normal way, jeans and a shirt would have sufficed, but
somehow the Villa Falcone demanded a less casual
approach. Or was it just Signora Vitale? she wondered shrewdly. Certainly, the old lady had not
approved of her slacks suit.

With a frown, she buttoned a green shirt across
her pointed breasts and stepped into a printed cotton
skirt, that swung in pleats against bare slender legs.
She refused to wear tights when it was so warm,
and stepping into cork-soled sandals, she brushed
vigorously at her straight hair. It swung in bleached
strands about her shoulders, and as an added adorn-
ment, she looped a heavy gold medallion on its chain
around her neck. She wore little make-up during the
day. Just a light foundation to prevent her skin from
shining, and mascara to add lustre to her already
dark lashes.

Before leaving the room, she approached the bed
again and looked down at the rose still lying on the
tray. She stretched out her hand towards it and then

withdrew it again, quickly. Whatever game Mazzaro
di Falcone was playing, she wanted no part of it, and
the rose could be returned to its owner without her
being involved. Even so, it troubled her that by his
action, Mazzaro had disrupted the even composure
she had always maintained, even in the face of Abdul
Fezik's pursuit, and made her more aware of him as
a man than anyone else she had ever met. But it was
ridiculous, she told herself severely, drawing in a
jerky breath. She was making far too much of what to
him had probably been nothing more than a mocking
gesture to the romanticism of his race. If she hadn't
glimpsed him walking in the courtyard hours before
she might not have thought anything about it.

But she left the rose on the tray when she went
downstairs.

There was a curving marble staircase leading down
into the main body of the hall, its ornate handrail
an example of baroque ironwork. The night before,
Suzanne had been able to see little of the beauty of
this part of the villa, shrouded in darkness as it had
been, but now she could see the domed ceiling overhead, and the round windows casting prisms of light
in many colours over the mosaic tiling of the floor.
The acoustics in the hall were such that she could
even hear the sound of her cork-soled feet on the
stair, and the rustle of her skirt against her legs.

The magnificent doors at the front of the villa
were closed at present, but she guessed that when
the building was opened to the public, visitors would
come in that way and get the full benefit from their
first glimpse of that nave-like entrance.

Tempted to linger and study the building in more detail, Suzanne walked determinedly across the hall and turned into the wing of the building occupied by the family. Perhaps later, she could ask Pietro if she might explore, but for the present she was a guest in the house and not a tourist.

The doors to the small salon were closed, and she was hesitating about opening them, when she heard the sound of steel against marble and the dragging sound of feet being propelled with effort. She knew at once who it was, and her head jerked round nervously as Mazzaro di Falcone approached her along the gallery. This morning, the sombreness of his attire was relieved somewhat by a dark red shirt, but his pants were still uncompromisingly black.

Seen in broad daylight, the scars on the right side of his face were a network of dry tissue, unhealthily white against the deeply tanned pigment of his skin. Suzanne's eyes were drawn to them almost against her will, and she had to force herself to look away.

'Good morning, Miss Hunt,' he greeted her in English, inclining his head forward. 'I trust you slept well.'

Suzanne had to look at him then, but the bland green eyes revealed no trace of its being a barbed question. 'I—it was very hot,' she compromised. 'But I was very comfortable, thank you, Count.'

'That is good.' Without removing his hands from the sticks, he gestured towards the doors of the room he had first emerged from the night before. 'Perhaps you will join me for coffee? If you would open the doors. . .'

It was a command, more than a request, and as Suzanne did not know her way about well enough to demur, she moved forward automatically and taking hold of the iron handles, swung the doors inward.

The room beyond was booklined and comfortable, as she had seen in passing the night before, but with a square mahogany desk, presently untidy with files and papers, and leather chairs in keeping with its use as a study. Of all the rooms in the villa she had entered so far, it was the least aggressively impressive, and possessed a charm and intimacy lacking in those larger apartments.

Mazzaro propelled himself into the room, and indicated that she should close the doors behind them. She did so reluctantly, impatient with herself unjustifiably for getting into such a position. Perhaps she should have stayed in her room until Pietro returned and came looking for her. But how could she have known that Mazzaro di Falcone would feel obliged to entertain her in Pietro's absence?

She closed the doors and leaned back against them for a moment, her eyes moving to the long windows which gave an uninterrupted view of the fountain in the courtyard. But as yet these glass doors were closed, and there was no escape that way.

Mazzaro was regarding her with a disturbing scrutiny that increased her own feelings of unease, and she realised she had never encountered this kind of situation before. The conviction grew in her that she was to blame, that she was reading more into his behaviour because of her own peculiar reactions to

him, which was ridiculous when she seriously
thought about it. In the course of her work, she had
met dozens of men, and many of them had shown
her friendliness and admiration. She had met handsome men, rich men, charming men—men of all
ages and nationalities; and it was positively ludicrous
for her to feel this way about a middle-aged Italian
count, who dragged himself around on two sticks
and whose face would terrify small children.

'Does my disfigurement repel you, Miss Hunt?'
Mazzaro asked now, and she guessed he had misread
the emotions that played so revealingly across
her face.

'No,' she said at once, colouring like a schoolgirl
speaking to a superior. 'Not at all.'

'No?' He sounded sceptical. 'Yet you are reluctant
to be alone with me, Miss Hunt.'

His candour disconcerted her further. 'No. I—why
I was just wondering when Pietro would be back. . .'

Mazzaro's dark brows ascended. 'Indeed.' He gestured towards one of the leather chairs set beside the
desk. 'Well, not yet, at any rate, so won't you sit
down, Miss Hunt? Or would you rather remain
poised for flight? I promise you, in any race between
us, you would win.'

Her face flushed, Suzanne moved away from the
door and took the chair he offered, crossing her legs
and then uncrossing them again when she realised
that by so doing she was exposing the smooth skin
of her thigh. If Mazzaro noticed this small charade,
he made no comment upon it, moving round his desk
to take the chair opposite her. He seated himself

slowly, setting the sticks aside, immediately assuming that air of command he had possessed at dinner the evening before.

For a few moments he seemed content to relax, his hands resting loosely over the arms of the chair. His hands were brown, and long-fingered, a jewelled signet ring on his left hand catching the light as it moved. Suzanne fixed her gaze no higher than his desk. As well as the mass of papers upon it, there was an onyx paperweight, and a gold inkstand, and a bronze statuette of a bull, which must surely be very old. Her hands itched to hold the statuette. The metal looked very smooth, burnished to a dull shine, cool to the touch. She wanted to hold it between her palms and feel the metal expand beneath the probing caress of her fingers. . .

'Have you known my cousin long, Miss Hunt?'

Mazzaro's question interrupted her train of thought, and her head came up jerkily. His eyes were narrowed as they watched her, cat-like between the thick short lashes. For a moment, she almost believed he had known what she was thinking and deliberately broken the thread.

'Wh-what?' she stammered. 'Oh, no—no. Not long.'

'How long?'

'I'm not sure exactly. About two months, I suppose.'

'Not long, as you say.' He brought his elbow to rest on the arm of his chair, supporting his chin with the knuckles of one hand. 'How well would you say you know Pietro?'

'How well?' Suzanne shifted awkwardly under his gaze. 'As well as anyone knows anyone else after such a short space of time, I imagine.'

'You think time is relative to how well one knows another person?'

'Well—of course.' Suzanne hesitated. 'Don't you?'

He did not answer, for at that moment there came a knock at the study door, and Suzanne looked round in relief. But at his command, it was Lucia who entered with the coffee he must have ordered earlier. There was only one cup, however, and in swift Italian he requested that she fetch another.

Suzanne was uncomfortably aware that Lucia had given her a swift appraisal as she came into the room, and no doubt she was speculating on the relationship between Pietro's English friend and the lord of Castelfalcone.

While the old servant went to get a second cup, Mazzaro poured coffee for one, raising the cream jug in silent interrogation. But Suzanne mutely shook her head, adding two spoons of sugar when he pushed the cup towards her. She lifted the cup and saucer into her hands, stirring it vigorously, and then stopping herself from doing so when she found mocking green eyes upon her.

Lucia returned a few moments later, and Mazzaro thanked her warmly. 'It was my pleasure, *signore*,' she responded, with a knowing smile. 'If there is anything else. . .'

'We will let you know, Lucia. Thank you.'

Mazzaro inclined his head and Lucia made her

departure, the smile still on her lips.

Suzanne looked down into her coffee cup. This was the moment she should ask him why he had put the rose on her tray, she thought fiercely. He must know he was giving Lucia a deliberately false impression of their association, and heaven knew what she might make of it. Summoning all her determination, she looked up and found his eyes upon her.

'*Signore*—' she was beginning, when he said abruptly: 'I saw you admiring my statuette. Do you know anything about such objects, Miss Hunt?'

Suzanne's momentary resolution fled. 'It—it's bronze, isn't it?' she ventured, and despised herself for her weakness. 'Is it Italian?'

His smile was wry. 'I am afraid not, Miss Hunt.' He picked up the small statuette, and smoothed it between his fingers as she had wanted to do. 'This little fellow was made in Egypt many, many centuries ago. It is bronze, as you say, but many of these antiquities were imported from Greece or North Africa. The Romans themselves, I regret to say, did not appear to have had an innate capacity for art. Nevertheless, they were sufficiently well educated to recognise and appreciate articles of artistic merit.'

Suzanne found herself leaning forward. 'It—it must be very valuable,' she murmured.

'It is without price,' he stated, without conceit. 'To a collector like myself, such objects defy valuation.' He extended his hand across the desk. 'Would you like to examine it?'

Suzanne stared at him aghast. 'But I—I'd be afraid—I might drop it!'

Mazzaro's full lower lip curved almost sensuously. 'I trust you not to do that,' he remarked, gesturing with the bronze. 'Go ahead. Take it.'

Once more his words were in the nature of a command, and setting down her cup and saucer, she took the statuette from his hand. The exchange was executed without their fingers touching, but the bronze was still warm from his flesh.

It was a solid little article, standing squarely on an inch-thick base, probably used to decorate some wealthy Egyptian's home thousands of years before. The animal's head was lowered slightly, as if ready to charge, its horns projecting wickedly.

'Aren't you afraid someone might steal it?' she exclaimed, looking up at him, forcing herself to return his stare.

Mazzaro shrugged. 'I should be sorry if he disappeared, naturally,' he said. 'But sometimes I wonder whether I am right to hold on to such an object. Why should I be permitted to possess something which is, in fact, no more mine than anyone else's?'

'But your family must have owned it—'

'—for many years. Yes, I know,' he agreed dryly. 'But that does not alter the situation. No doubt my ancestors were no better than profiteers, taking advantage of those less knowledgeable than themselves.'

Suzanne looked down at the statuette, stroking the arc of its tail. 'Not everyone appreciates such things.'

'Are you defending my ancestors—or my honour, Miss Hunt?'

Suzanne moved her shoulders impatiently. 'I'm sure that whatever you say, you would not like to think of him in the hands of some unfeeling dealer,' she persisted. She looked up. 'Would you?'

Mazzaro's eyes shifted to her hands, moving lovingly over the heavy object. 'It would seem that already my selfishness has been rewarded,' he commented. 'Will you be as sympathetic to everything that is mine, Miss Hunt?'

His words had a dual edge, and she leant forward quickly and replaced the small bull on his desk. She wished he would not say such things to her. She wished she was not affected by them as she was. Of what possible interest could her approval be to him?

'Now what is wrong, Miss Hunt?' he inquired, as her eyes sought the open spaces of the courtyard. 'If it is of any consolation to you, the insurance company demands that I seal the gates electrically at night. Then we have installed an ultrasonic sound-wave transmitter. Any movement by an intruder distorts the waves coming to the receiver, and triggers an alarm system on the premises.'

Suzanne frowned. 'A sort of—neonic beam?'

'No. This is a more sophisticated system. Beams can be avoided. Sound-waves cannot.'

'I see.'

Suzanne was impressed. All the same, she had opened her balcony doors the night before without experiencing any difficulty. Couldn't an intruder enter that way? She shivered involuntarily. She would make sure she closed the doors in future.

'You are frowning, Miss Hunt.' Mazzaro reached for his sticks and got to his feet again, and Suzanne had to steel herself to remain where she was. 'Are you perhaps concerned about something?'

Suzanne bit her lip. Here was her chance again. Was she to let it slip a second time. 'I—I was wondering what—what would happen if some member of the—household happened to forget about the alarm system and—and stepped outside?'

Mazzaro came round the desk towards her, his eyes disturbingly intent. 'You mean, as you did last night, Miss Hunt?' he queried softly, and she gazed up at him in dismay, the initiative taken out of her grasp.

'You—you know?' she stammered.

'That you were walking on your balcony at two o'clock this morning? Yes, I know, Miss Hunt.'

Suzanne could feel the back of her neck growing damp. 'But then—you must know that I—that I—'

'—saw me walking without these?' He lifted one of the sticks from the floor. 'Yes, Miss Hunt.'

Suzanne wished she could get up, but to do so would bring her that much closer to Mazzaro di Falcone, and right now he was quite close enough. 'I'm afraid I don't understand,' she murmured faintly.

'No.' He inclined his head. 'How could you?'

'Don't you need those sticks at all?' she cried.

'Not now. Not really. Although there are occasions when I am tired and walking is an effort.'

Suzanne pressed her lips together for a moment.

'But—don't you care that I know? Why did you let me see?'

He shrugged. 'It wasn't deliberate. The alarm sounded on the panel beside my bed. I had stepped into the courtyard before I realised what it must be. After that, I had to reassure myself.'

'But if it had been burglars!' she protested, and he half smiled.

'Your concern is touching, Miss Hunt, but I was armed.'

Her skin prickled. 'You don't want me to—to tell Pietro?'

'I can't stop you from doing so.'

'But why haven't you done so yourself? Surely your wife would be delight—'

But something in his sudden stiffening made her realise she had gone too far. 'My wife's feelings need not concern you, Miss Hunt,' he stated harshly, moving away from her again. He had not straightened or attempted to walk without the aid of the sticks, and the ridiculous notion came to her that whatever he said she had imagined the whole thing.

'Would—would you rather I kept this knowledge to myself, then?' she probed, as he halted by the long windows, his back towards her.

He was silent for so long, she had begun to think he could not have heard her, when he said quietly: 'Let us say I have my reasons for remaining silent at this time, Miss Hunt. However, if you feel you cannot keep my secret, I will not reproach you for it.'

Suzanne pushed back her chair and got to her feet, linking her fingers tightly together. 'Why did you

send me the rose, *signore?*' she ventured, finding the
question easier than she had expected.

He turned then, more lithely than he could have
done had the sticks been needed, and surveyed her
with a wryly mocking amusement. 'Of course. It was
presumptuous of me, was it not?' he conceded. 'That
a man like myself should overstep the bounds of his
limitations and show himself vulnerable to admiration for a beautiful woman!'

Suzanne took a deep breath. 'I don't know what
you mean.'

'I may be disabled, Miss Hunt, but I am not blind.
And besides, I wanted us to have this talk, which
has proved most satisfactory, I think.'

'But. . .' Suzanne hesitated. 'What has your—
appearance to do with whether or not you sent me
a rose?'

Mazzaro's expression hardened. 'Please do not
insult me by pretending naïveté,' he retorted stiffly.

Suzanne sighed. 'I'm sorry if you think I was being
insulting. I just don't happen to see the connection
between the two.' She paused. 'I don't believe that
a person's appearance has a great deal of bearing on
their personality.'

'Your inexperience is showing, Miss Hunt,' he
returned cynically, but his features were less severe.
'You will find that appearances count for a lot. A
beautiful woman has the confidence that a less
favoured contemporary has not. Looks frequently
determine an individual's course in life, and those
less fortunate often become morose and bitter.' He

shrugged eloquently. 'Like roses, we are judged on our overall composition, no?'

'No!' Suzanne was vehement. 'You are not morose and bitter!'

'And you think I should be?'

'No!' Too late, she had realised what she was saying. 'I—I should feel sorry for someone who—who deserved—'

'Pity?' He inserted, as she hesitated once more. 'But you don't think I deserve pity, is that it?'

Suzanne looked across at him uncertainly, aware of the cleft stick into which he had steered her. 'No,' she said at last, slowly and distinctly. 'I don't feel sorry for you, Count di Falcone.'

There was a moment's silence, and her conscience pricked her. Had she been unnecessarily harsh? Had he taken offence at her clumsily-worded beliefs?

'Very well, Miss Hunt,' he said finally, moving to prop himself against the side of his desk. He shifted both sticks into one hand and raked long fingers through the thick vitality of his hair. The action parted the collar of his shirt, revealing more of the savage scarring. 'So now we know where we stand, do we not?'

Suzanne's tangled emotions made it difficult for her to reply. She had the feeling that something was happening to her here, over which she had no control. It was as if she was seeing herself through a glass screen, aware of the dangers of becoming involved with this man, but unable to reach out and prevent the inevitable happening. . .

CHAPTER THREE

THE sudden opening of the door was both a relief and an intrusion.

Suzanne turned away from the man as his daughter came into the room, pale and foreign-looking in her neat silk dress, a wide-brimmed bonnet dangling by its ribbons from her hand.

'Papà—' she was beginning, only to halt uncertainly at the sight of Suzanne standing uncomfortably in the middle of the floor.

Mazzaro transferred the sticks to his hands, and straightened away from the desk, achieving his usual posture as Lucia followed the child into the room.

'Elena!' she scolded in Italian, 'how many times have I told you not to enter your father's study without first knocking? *Signore*—'

'That is all right, Lucia.' Mazzaro shook his head at the elderly servant. 'You may leave us. I gather my aunt is home from church.'

'Yes, *signore*.' Lucia nodded, flicking a quick glance at Suzanne and away again. 'You would like more coffee?'

'Thank you, no, Lucia,' Mazzaro declined, and with a reluctant bob, she left them.

Elena stood just inside the doorway, twisting the brim of her bonnet round and round in her hands, and Suzanne wished she could think of something

to say to the child. It was obvious she was ill at ease,
but whether that was wholly to do with Suzanne's
presence, or in part due to her father's expected cen-
sure, she could not be sure.

'Have you been introduced to Miss Hunt, Elena?'
Mazzaro spoke in English as the door closed, and
the child stole a dark-eyed glance at Suzanne. But
she did not reply.

'Elena and I introduced ourselves yesterday
evening.' Suzanne felt obliged to speak. 'Didn't
we, Elena?'

Still the child remained silent, swinging her hat
against the full skirt of her dress, scuffing her toes
against each other.

'Elena!'

Mazzaro's voice had become a little impatient
now, and the little girl looked at him anxiously.
'*Si*, Papà?'

'I asked whether you had been introduced to Miss
Hunt, Elena?'

Elena chewed on her lower lip. '*No*, Papà.'

Suzanne sighed. 'Is this necessary?' she
exclaimed. 'Elena was with your aunt last evening.'

Mazzaro looked at her coolly. 'But you were not
introduced to my daughter?'

'Not formally, no.' Suzanne clenched her fists and
walked towards the door. 'If you will excuse me,
signore. . . Your aunt is back from church and no
doubt Pietro is, too.'

'One moment, Miss Hunt.'

His power to command frightened her, and she
reached for the handle of the door blindly, deter-

mined not to be intimidated by him. But he moved
swiftly across the room, belying the use of his sticks
to a discerning eye, and laid a detaining hand on her
arm. The stick he had been holding clattered on to
the floor, and Elena darted forward anxiously to
retrieve it for him. Suzanne wondered what she must
be thinking, seeing her father apparently supporting
himself on the arm of a stranger, but even she could
not be aware of the pain he was perhaps involuntarily
inflicting.

'What will you say to Pietro, Miss Hunt?' he
demanded, and Suzanne drew her arm away in relief
as Elena handed him the stick.

'I am only here for a few days, *signore*,' she managed tautly, rubbing the circulation back into her
arm. 'I shan't interfere.'

And before he could detain her further, she let
herself quickly out of the door.

She walked on rather uncertain legs along the coolly
lofty hall to the door through which she and Pietro
had entered the villa the evening before, and jerking
it open, emerged into the brilliance of the day.

The light was dazzling, but the sense of release
she was experiencing was intoxicating. She breathed
deeply of the wine-like air, and then stepped out on
to the mosaic tiling of the courtyard.

The fountain drew her like a magnet, the play
of water on marble reflecting the sun in a hundred
different globules of light. She leant on the basin,
admiring the classic figure of a nymph, modestly
clutching her falling draperies about her, and trailed

her fingers in the spray. She didn't look towards the
windows which she knew belonged to Mazzaro's
study, but still she was conscious of eyes
watching her.

With a feeling of frustration, she swung round,
only to confront a blank wall of glass. There was no
one watching her from Mazzaro's study, and she felt
rather foolish. She was turning away again when a
movement just above her head attracted her attention.
She looked up—straight into the curiously tight-
lipped features of Sophia di Falcone.

'Oh!' Suzanne couldn't prevent the small exclamation that escaped her, while her eyes registered
that Sophia was clearly not long out of bed, her cap
of bronze hair rumpled, her silk wrapper revealing
that she wore little beneath it. '*Buon giorno*,
Contessa.'

'*Buon giorno*, Miss Hunt.' Sophia rapidly recovered from the impression Suzanne had received that
she was not pleased about being observed watching
their guest. 'Are you a worshipper of Aphrodite?'

'Aphrodite?' Suzanne blinked, and then with comprehension, glanced back at the fountain. 'Oh, you
mean the statue. . .'

'I am sure Aphrodite would not care to be
described as such,' commented Sophia dryly. 'A
statue implies a remoteness, a sense of being placed
on a pedestal, beyond reach. The followers of
Aphrodite would reject such an image, I am sure.'

Suzanne had no intention of being drawn into a
discussion on this subject. Having just escaped from
one tense situation, she had no wish to create another.

Taking a deep breath, she said: 'It's a beautiful morning, isn't it?'

Sophia's lips drooped, apparently disappointed that Suzanne had changed the subject. 'I have seen many such mornings, *signorina*,' she retorted, and with an imperious gesture, she disappeared across the balcony and into the room behind her. Her bedroom? Suzanne wondered, and then dismissed the suggestion. It was no concern of hers where Sophia di Falcone slept. And yet she did not think that the aristocratic Contessa shared her husband's bed. She was disgusted at the emotions that stirred within her at this realisation. . .

She looked back at the fountain. The bland marble eyes of the goddess seemed to mock her reluctant mood of introspection, and almost desperately she brushed past the rim of the basin and walked towards the box hedges encircling a smooth lawn.

'So there you are, Suzanne! I've been looking everywhere for you.'

Suzanne had never expected to find Pietro's young voice so appealing. He came strolling out of the villa, slim and boyish, in casual slacks and a floral shirt, and she turned towards him almost eagerly.

'Have you, Pietro?'

'Yes.' Pietro spoke in his own language. 'Mamma wishes you to take chocolate with her.' He smiled. 'You missed me?'

Suzanne could have wished they were going to spend some time alone, but to voice such a suggestion to Pietro was to invite the wrong kind of reactions. So instead she returned his smile and

answered: 'Lucia told me you had gone to Mass. I'm
sorry I wasn't awake to go with you.'

Pietro urged her back towards the villa. 'I did not
think you would want to go,' he said honestly. 'But
I am glad you slept so well. Sometimes it is not easy
to sleep in a strange bed, but I suppose in your work
you are used to it.'

Suzanne felt a surge of almost hysterical amusement rising inside her. It was good to relax again.
She had been taking everything that had happened
far too seriously. But the extent of her hysteria
revealed the tension she had experienced.

'I—I shouldn't let anyone else hear you say that,'
she choked, and they were laughing together as they
entered the small salon where Signora Vitale was
waiting for them.

Lucia served chocolate and sweet biscuits, and
although Suzanne would have preferred something
cooler, she politely acknowledged the old lady's hos-
pitality. Lucia permitted herself a conspiratorial
glance in her direction. She seemed to be thriving
on what she imagined was an intriguing situation,
and Suzanne silently berated Mazzaro for creating
this entirely misleading impression. But the old servant's speculation successfully deprived her of the
sense of perspective she had achieved, and she
nibbled uneasily at a biscuit wondering whether all
Italian households were as complex.

Pietro, however, seemed to notice nothing amiss.
He and his mother had obviously plenty to say to
one another after their weeks of separation, but they

included Suzanne in their conversation, and she eventually relaxed again.

Sophia appeared just as Pietro had offered to show Suzanne the gardens of the villa. She sauntered into the room, smoothly soignée in flared white pants and a bronze halter top, a printed silk scarf knotted casually about her throat. She kissed Signora Vitale, touched Pietro's cheek with a lingering intimacy, and smiled at Suzanne. There was no trace left of the petulant woman who had withdrawn from her balcony half an hour before.

'I am going out, Zia Tommasa,' she addressed Pietro's mother, but Pietro uttered a disappointed protest. 'I must, *caro*,' she added, turning to him. 'I have promised. You know how it is.'

'But this is my first day home, Sophia,' he reproached, and she stroked his cheek once more, her eyes moving with a certain amount of satisfaction over his pale features.

'You are here for many days, Pietro *mio*,' she intoned, her eyes full of promise, and Suzanne was made uncomfortably aware that their relationship was as ambiguous as everything else here. Had this anything to do with Mazzaro's attitude towards his wife? Surely not! Sophia must be almost ten years older than her husband's cousin!

Suzanne suddenly realised that Pietro's mother was watching their interchange equally as distastefully. Did she have her suspicions about their relationship, too? Or did she just dislike Sophia's proprietorial attitude towards her son?

Sophia moved away from Pietro then, towards the

door. 'We'll meet again at dinner, Miss Hunt,' she said, casting another smile in Suzanne's direction. '*Arrivederci*, Zia Tommasa. *Arrivederci*, Pietro.'

'Sophia spends too much time away from the villa,' grumbled Signora Vitale, as the sound of her heels receded along the hall. She looked impatiently at her son. 'And you should not encourage her.'

Pietro's cheeks flamed with colour, and Suzanne's feelings changed rapidly to sympathy for him. He was a young man, after all, not a boy, and his mother had no right to humiliate him like this in front of a guest.

Getting to her feet, she said determinedly: 'You were going to show me the gardens, weren't you, Pietro?' and he turned to her gratefully.

'Yes, I was,' he agreed. 'You will excuse us, won't you, Mamma?'

Walking along the stone-paved path between neatly clipped hedges, Suzanne glanced doubtfully at her companion. Pietro had said little since they left the villa, and she wondered whether he was thinking about Sophia, or his mother's condemnation. Whatever it was that was occupying his thoughts was not pleasing him, and on impulse, she said:

'How did your cousin have his accident?'

Pietro looked at her uncomprehendingly for a moment, and then he pulled himself together. 'Mazzaro?' he said, and she heard the hardening of his tone. 'He fell off a cliff.'

'A cliff!' Suzanne was aghast. 'But how—'

'Skiing,' replied Pietro shortly. 'He used to be an excellent skier.'

'Oh!' Suzanne frowned. She had imagined a car accident, something like that.

'He used to spend weeks at Cortina,' remarked Pietro dourly. 'Until he fell. Now he never goes near the place.'

'You can't blame him for that,' murmured Suzanne with feeling, and Pietro sent her a sharp look.

'Why not?' he demanded. 'He was drunk when the accident happened. He should never have been out on the slopes. He wouldn't have fallen in the normal way—he was far too clever for that.'

'How can you be sure?' Suzanne stared at him. 'You're so callous! He could have been killed!'

'Has he found himself a defendant?' Pietro's lips twisted. 'Suzanne, it would have been simpler for every—'

'No!' Suzanne interrupted him fiercely. 'Don't say it. Don't even think such things. Just because you don't agree with the way he's trying to hold on to his heritage—'

'His heritage!' Pietro was scathing. 'Inanimate objects! This place is a museum. My cousin is the most selfish man I know, Suzanne. You've seen how he behaves—how he treats his wife. Surely you can't condone that!'

Suzanne bent her head, unwilling to let Pietro see how his words affected her. What he said was true— about Sophia, at least. But there were usually two sides to every argument. As for Mazzaro's motives in opening his house to the public, she had some sympathy with them. Why should he sell things he obviously cared about when he was able to support himself and his family on the proceeds from allowing interested, and admittedly inquisitive, tourists to view them? After their conversation this morning, she felt instinctively that Mazzaro welcomed the opportunity to share his delight in the treasures he possessed. And that was not a selfish attitude.

Not answering his question, she said: 'How badly was he hurt—when he fell, I mean?' and Pietro made an impatient sound.

'How badly?' he repeated. 'Do you want a list of his injuries?' He snorted. 'Well, he broke both his legs and fractured his spine. He was in a wheelchair for over a year after he came out of hospital.'

'And. . .and the scarring. . .'

Pietro sighed. 'Friction causes heat, Suzanne. Don't make me go into details.' He ran his fingers through his hair irritatedly. 'I'm not inhuman—I know he must have suffered agonies. But that doesn't excuse his behaviour towards Sophia—or the way he's mean with her. You ought to know the size of the pitiable allowance he makes her.'

Suzanne raised her hands to loop her hair back behind her ears, and allowed them to rest against the sides of her neck. It was unforgivable, but she found she didn't much care about Sophia's allowance. Her skin was tingling at the horrifying images Pietro's earlier words had created. What bloody wreck of a man had been brought down from the mountains at Cortina, Italy's most fashionable skiing resort? What had Sophia's reactions been when she first under-stood the extent of her husband's injuries?

Suddenly she realised that Pietro was looking at her, and with a little shrug of her shoulders, she dismissed the shiver that had rippled down her spine. Dropping her hands to her sides, she looked determinedly about her, relieved when she caught sight of a vine-covered arbour and was able to ask what it was.

Pietro hesitated only a moment before accepting her sudden change of mood, and then replied: 'Mazzaro's mother designed it. It is what you would probably call a summer-house, *no*? I believe she used it as a retreat during the war when the villa was occupied by the military.'

Suzanne was intrigued. 'The villa was occupied?'

'All large villas were used by officers of the High Command as their headquarters,' Pietro explained. 'This happened in England, too, did it not?'

Suzanne nodded. 'Yes, of course.'

'My uncle was fortunate that the commandant was a civilised man. Many art treasures were destroyed or looted at that time.'

They had reached the stone steps leading into the arbour, and pushing aside the screening vines, Suzanne went inside. There was a musty smell of age and rotting vegetation. No one had troubled to ventilate the place, and creepers had overgrown the fluted columns. A stone bench circled the lower walls, but it had become a home of insects, and there were cobwebs everywhere.

'Is Mazz—is your cousin's mother dead?' Suzanne asked, as Pietro tore a clump of vines out by the roots and peered in at her.

'Yes,' he nodded. 'My uncle was killed when the plane he was piloting came down in the Alps in 1968, and she suffered a heart attack from which she never recovered. She died some six months later.'

'How awful for—for your cousin.'

'Mmm.' Pietro frowned. 'He and Sophia were living in Rome at the time his father was killed. Mazzaro was in his element, working for one of the great auction houses.'

Suzanne came to the head of the steps. 'Antique auctions?' she queried.

'Naturally. My cousin is a Professor of Antiquities, didn't you know?' Then he sighed. 'No, of course. How could you? I'm sorry, Suzanne. It seems that every time we talk about my cousin, I end up being rude to you.'

Suzanne came slowly down the steps, accepting the assistance of his hand as a gesture of apology. 'It's a shame no one cares about the arbour,' she murmured, glancing back at it regretfully.

Pietro shrugged. 'Luigi has enough to do, keeping the gardens tidy for the visitors.' He kicked an unoffending pebble viciously. 'That's what's wrong with this place. Too much to do, and no money to do it with!'

Suzanne wetted her upper lip with the tip of her tongue. 'Surely Lucia can't be responsible for the cleaning of the whole villa!' she exclaimed.

'Not in the tourist season, no,' he conceded. 'Mazzaro permits her to hire girls from the village to help with the polishing and sweeping. But he handles all the most valuable things himself. It's a full time job keeping everything in order,' he added irritably.

'And what would you have him do?' Suzanne questioned quietly, falling into step beside him again.

Pietro made a sweeping gesture. 'Me? I'd sell it all, *everything*! Do you realise, the contents of this place could keep us all in luxury for the rest of our lives!'

'And afterwards?' Suzanne prompted.

'Afterwards?' Pietro was uncomprehending.

'Yes, afterwards. After you are all dead.' Suzanne looked at him. 'Capital doesn't last for ever. Besides, what about your cousin's children—his grand-children?'

Pietro sneered. 'There's only Elena.'

'Well, she may marry one day and have children of her own. Would you deprive them of the chance to enjoy all this?'

'*Dio mio!*' Pietro raised his eyes heavenward. 'You talk like *he* does! Who can tell what might happen before Elena grows into a woman? There could be a war—a holocaust! We might none of us survive. Today is what matters, not some nebulous time in the future.'

'I don't agree.' Suzanne shook her head. 'If these things were disposed of—sold to various collectors who shut their valuables away in bank vaults, they'd never be seen again. You can't condone that. At least here, people can come and look—'

Pietro looked aghast. 'And you think that is right?'

Suzanne coloured. 'Well, I can see the justice of

it,' she admitted reluctantly. 'And I know that what you are suggesting is wrong.'

'Why? Surely it is wrong for one person to own so much?'

Suzanne sighed. 'It's not as simple as that, Pietro.'

'Is it not?' His mouth drooped sulkily. 'Has my cousin used my absence this morning to enlist your support? You were not his ally yesterday.'

He was more accurate than he knew, and this knowledge made her feel guilty. 'Allies!' she exclaimed frustratedly. 'Don't be silly, Pietro.'

'What is silly?' Pietro's eyes narrowed. 'I know my cousin better than you do, Suzanne. He has always had the—what do you call it?—the *charisma, no*? The appeal for your sex!'

'Pietro, you're being ridiculous—'

'Why? Deny to me that you are defending him!'

Suzanne was glad to reach the shadows of the loggia. 'What time is lunch?' she asked, as they entered the villa, refusing to continue with the argument, and after a moment, Pietro gave a shamefaced grimace of a smile.

'You see!' he said. 'We cannot discuss Mazzaro without anger.'

'We'll have to agree to differ,' Suzanne forced a light tone. 'I think I'll go and take a shower. I feel sticky after pushing through those vines.'

'Very well. Lunch is at two o'clock,' said Pietro, leaving her to enter the small salon. 'You know where the dining room is.'

'Yes.'

Suzanne nodded and left him, walking quickly

towards the main hall. As she ran up the wide marble staircase, and trod the corridor to her room, she determinedly tried to put all thoughts of Mazzaro di Falcone out of her mind.

Her bed had been made in her absence, and the contents of her suitcase put away in the cedar-lined drawers of a small chest. She supposed she had Lucia to thank for this, but left to herself, she would not have bothered to unpack the rest of her belongings. Somehow leaving them in the suitcase increased the feeling of her impermanence, a feeling she needed to preserve in these surroundings.

Before taking a shower, however, she pushed open the balcony doors and stepped to the rail. The courtyard below was deserted; the whole villa seemed to be drowsing in the noonday heat. The back of her neck prickled, but still she lingered, her gaze straying down the valley to where a village nestled lower on the hillside. A church bell was tolling somewhere, and its sound was muted and somnolent on the still air.

With a sigh, she turned away, and as she did so, she noticed that the rooms across the courtyard, which opened on to the opposite balcony, were all closed and shuttered, long blinds concealing their shadowy depths from prying eyes. The downstairs rooms, which she guessed Mazzaro opened to the public, were less ghostlike, and she realised they would have to be opened and aired every day.

It seemed impossible to keep thoughts of the man who owned the Villa Falcone out of her head, and she ran her shower more coldly and vigorously than usual, trying to numb the unwilling emotions he roused. She tried to imagine how she would have felt about him if he had come as a guest to one of the hotels where she had been working. In the course of her duties she had encountered men, and women, with disabilities of all kinds, but the amazing thing was, with Mazzaro di Falcone, she seldom thought about his. Whatever his failings, he was a man, in every sense of the word, both mentally and physically. . .

CHAPTER FOUR

SUZANNE did not see either Mazzaro or Sophia again
that day. At lunch, there were only four people at
table—herself and Pietro, Signora Vitale, and Elena.

Suzanne couldn't help feeling curious about Elena.
She was an abnormally well-behaved child, of
course, as children of her background sometimes
were, and living in a house of adults could not help.
But surely Elena was more withdrawn than usual for
a girl of her age, speaking only when spoken to, and
then in monosyllables. The only spark of excitement
Suzanne had seen was on their arrival the previous
evening, and then Signora Vitale had quickly extinguished it. She would have liked to have talked with
the child, discovered her likes and dislikes, and she
was still young enough to find the prospect of a game
of hide-and-seek played in these surroundings quite
appealing.

But Elena ate her food and disappeared for the
nap her father's aunt suggested, and any opportunity
of communicating with her was lost.

In the afternoon, Pietro took Suzanne down to the
village, and showed her the church where he and his
mother had attended Mass that morning. Like most
Italian churches, it possessed some exquisite sculp-
tures, and the ceiling paintings were particularly fine.

'I once read somewhere that the worshipper was

encouraged to raise his eyes to heaven, and through these paintings direct his senses towards the infinite,' remarked Suzanne, gazing upward. 'Do you find these impressions of the hereafter match your own?'

Pietro shrugged as they emerged into the sunlight again. 'I don't think I have any impressions of the hereafter,' he said. 'And you shouldn't believe everything you read.'

Suzanne smiled. 'All right, all right. But it did seem rather appropriate.' She paused. 'Pietro, does Elena rest every afternoon?'

He frowned. 'Elena? Well—yes, I believe so. Why?'

Suzanne draped the strap of her handbag over one shoulder. 'I was curious, that's all. And it did occur to me that we might take her out with us one day, if you didn't mind. She doesn't seem to get much fun out of life.'

'That's a subject you must take up with my cousin, not me,' retorted Pietro sharply, directing her along the narrow street towards the *piazza*. 'Much as I like the child, I have no intention of wasting our time together entertaining Elena.'

Suzanne was surprised at the vehemence of his tone. 'But, Pietro,' she exclaimed, 'why should having Elena along make any difference to us?'

Pietro halted, and turned to look into her wide brown eyes, unable to resist the appeal of honey-gold skin and softly parted lips. With an exclamation, he bent his head and pressed his mouth to hers, startling her into an unwilling response. 'That's why,' he told her huskily, and would have kissed her again except that Suzanne forestalled him by taking a quick backward step.

'Pietro!' she protested, looping her hair back behind her ears. 'That was not part of our arrangement.'

'Suzanne!' he exclaimed reproachfully. 'You're not going to pretend you don't know how I feel about you, are you?'

'I think we could both do with a cup of coffee,' she replied, and walked quickly along the street towards the square.

But as they sat at one of the tables under the trees, drinking cups of strong black coffee and listening to the chatter of Italian voices mingled with the muted sounds of an accordian, Suzanne hoped she was not going to be faced with problems of another kind.

Dinner was served late, and Elena did not join them.

'Mazzaro is dining with the Rossis,' Pietro's mother told her son, forking a mouthful of cured ham and following it by a cube of iced melon. 'Did you know that Marina was home again?'

Pietro shook his head. 'No. Is she staying long?'

Signora Vitale shrugged her thin shoulders. 'Your guess is as good as mine. Mazzaro says that she has been overdoing things, that she needs a rest. Her father is delighted to see her, of course. He misses her terribly when she is away.'

Suzanne lifted her wine glass and allowed the pale liquid it contained to touch her lips. Who were they talking about? she wondered. Who were the Rossis? And Marina in particular?

As if in answer to her silent question, Pietro turned to her then. 'The Rossis are friends of the family,' he explained. 'Mazzaro and Marina practically grew up together, although she is about five years younger than he is.' His lips tightened. 'My uncle expected they would marry one day, but Mazzaro had other plans at that time. He went to Rome and married Sophia, and Marina eventually took herself off to medical school and qualified as a doctor. Their positions are reversed now—she lives and works in Rome.'

'I see.' Suzanne replaced her glass on the table.

'Of course, it's arguable exactly what their present relationship is,' he was beginning, when his mother silenced him with an angry word of reproof.

'Please do not discuss such matters in public, Pietro!' she snapped impatiently. 'Keep your gutter gossip to yourself!'

Pietro flushed hotly. 'Mazzaro doesn't care about Sophia, Mamma. You know that as well as I do.'

'I know that your cousin's accident put a strain on all of us. Pietro—Sophia included.'

'You're suggesting that she's to blame?'

'I'm not suggesting anything,' retorted his mother quellingly. 'But as for implying that Mazzaro's friendship with Marina is anything more than that. . .' She shook her head. 'You would do well to keep your comments to yourself.'

Pietro's lips twitched resentfully, and Suzanne looked down uncomfortably at her plate. It could be argued that Pietro's defence of his cousin's wife bordered on jealousy, although she suspected that

Sophia accepted his admiration with more indulgence that enthusiasm. Nevertheless, it was not jealousy for Sophia which stirred like a snake in Suzanne's stomach. . .

The following morning, she was awake early. She had slept unexpectedly soundly, in spite of the turmoil of her thoughts, and she was up and dressed by eight o'clock. Following Sophia's example, she decided to disregard Signora Vitale's disapproval and wear pants, slim-fitting cotton flares, in an attractive shade of orange that teamed well with a green and white striped vest. The low neckline of the vest revealed the swell of her breasts, and she was pleased to see that already her arms were losing their paleness.

Deciding to go in search of breakfast, she went downstairs, enjoying the coolness of the air against her heated skin. Lucia was using an electric polisher along the hall, and she stared at Suzanne in surprise, switching off the machine.

'*Buon giorno, signorina,*' she exclaimed. '*Lei è mattiniero.*'

Suzanne smiled, and speaking in Italian said: 'Yes, I am early, Lucia. But don't let me disturb you.'

'Ah, *signorina*, you are not disturbing me. The *signore*, he is having breakfast at this moment. You can join him, no?'

Suzanne cleared her throat. 'The—the *signore*? You mean—the *Conte*?'

'Of course, *signorina*. He will be most happy to have company, yes?'

Suzanne hesitated. 'Really, I—I can wait. . .'

'No need, *signorina*. Go ahead. I will not be long.
She was cornered. Taking a deep breath, Suzanne
walked to the double doors of the dining room, and
after another moment's hesitation, tapped lightly on
the panels. She heard Mazzaro's attractively deep
voice bidding her in Italian to enter, and she pushed
open the doors.

Mazzaro was seated in his position at the head of
the long table. A dark green silk shirt gaped open at
his throat to reveal the darkly pigmented skin of his
chest, shadowed by fine dark hair, and Suzanne's
pulses quickened at the casual sensuality of the man.
A newspaper was propped against a coffee pot on
the table in front of him, and he did not look up from
its pages as he said: '*Niente più*, Lucia. *Grazie!*' But
he was not alone at the table. Elena was seated near to
her father, spreading conserve thickly over a golden
croissant, and she said quickly: '*Non è* Lucia, Papà!
bringing his head up with a jerk to confront
Suzanne's apologetic features.

'*Scusi, signore*,' she murmured awkwardly, wishing the floor would open up and swallow her, but
Mazzaro merely put down the cup he had been raising to his lips and endeavoured to lever himself up
out of his chair, supporting himself on the table.
'Good morning, Miss Hunt.'

'Oh, please. . .' Suzanne lapsed back into English
in her embarrassment. 'Don't get up, *signore*. I—
Lucia sent me in here. She said you would not object
if we—if I joined you for breakfast. . .'

Mazzaro gestured to the chair on his left, opposite
Elena. 'Lucia was right, for once,' he remarked

mockingly. 'We do not object if Miss Hunt joins us for breakfast, do we, Elena?

Elena shook her head, her expression unrevealing, and Suzanne closed the heavy doors and came quickly to the table, seating herself jerkily, relieved when he sank back into his chair again. When he stood over her, as momentarily he had been, his physical superiority was too marked—too disturbing.

'You do not sleep late, Miss Hunt,' he commented, folding the newspaper and laying it aside.

'I wish you wouldn't let my presence alter your routine, *signore*,' she murmured, glancing at Elena, who was continuing to eat her breakfast. 'Read your newspaper. I don't mind, honestly.'

'But what if I do?' he countered. 'Relax, Miss Hunt. There is nothing between these pages which cannot wait until later.' He poured himself more coffee. 'I assume Lucia is preparing your meal.'

'Yes.' Suzanne shifted restlessly. Then belatedly: 'Thank you.'

Mazzaro considered her anxious features. 'You spent a pleasant day yesterday, I trust?'

Suzanne forced a smile. 'Very pleasant, thank you.'

'Pietro took you out?'

'In the afternoon, yes. We went down to the village.'

'And what do you think of Castelfalcone?'

'I like it.' Suzanne moved her shoulders appreciatively. 'The church is quite beautiful.'

'Ah, yes. The church of San Lorenzo,' Mazzaro

nodded. 'Do you know about Gothic architecture, Miss Hunt?'

'I'm afraid not.' Suzanne smiled into Elena's solemn little face. 'I'm very ignorant.'

Mazzaro's lips twitched. 'Not at all. I know nothing about hotel management, but I do not consider that a crime.' He was evidently trying to put her at her ease. 'We have some outstanding examples of Gothic architecture in this country. The cathedral at Siena, for example. Naturally I would know of them.'

'As a Professor of Antiquities, you mean?' she ventured.

Mazzaro frowned. 'Now who would tell you that, I wonder?' he queried dryly, and she looked nervously down at her hands. 'Pietro, I suppose. Did he also tell you his opinion of my idea to open the Villa to the public?'

Suzanne longed for Lucia to appear with her breakfast. 'He—he may have mentioned something about it,' she admitted reluctantly, aware that Elena too was watching her now.

'How discreet you are, Miss Hunt.' Mazzaro's lips twisted. 'I am sure Pietro did more than mention his feelings to you. But no matter. I respect your desire to remain neutral. It would not be fair for me to cross-examine you about Pietro's somewhat right-wing views. He understands the value of the collection, of course, but he is a sybarite at heart, and this gets in the way of his objectivity.'

While Suzanne was trying to think of something innocuous to reply, Lucia at last appeared with fresh rolls and coffee, and more of the freshly-squeezed orange juice she had enjoyed the previous morning. The elderly servant seemed pleased that the *signore* had company for breakfast, but remembering the incident of the rose, Suzanne wondered what she really thought.

When Lucia had departed once more, and she was sipping at her orange juice, Mazzaro said quietly: 'What plans have you and Pietro for today, Miss Hunt?' and Suzanne looked up.

'I think the *signora*—Pietro's mother—expects him to take her to somewhere called Muvano this morning, *signore*,' she replied, and Elena broke her silence to say: '*Si*, Papà. Muvano!' before Suzanne added: 'And—and I wondered whether I might have your permission to look round the Villa, *signore*.'

Mazzaro's dark brows drew together, accentuating the occasionally malevolent cast of his features, and for a moment she thought she had offended him. But his next words reassured her on that point.

'Surely Zia Tommasa could wait until his girl-friend returns to London before involving Pietro in her social meanderings!' he exclaimed with asperity. 'Yesterday it was Mass, today it is Muvano, what will it be tomorrow, I wonder?' He made an exasperated sound. 'Mass again, I suppose.'

'I don't mind, really.' Suzanne reached for the coffee pot, steadying it with both hands. 'I mean. . .' she met his gaze uneasily, '. . .it was kind of Pietro to invite me here to join his family for the weekend, but—well, we're just friends, you know. Not—

not engaged, or anything. He isn't obliged to entertain me.'

Mazzaro regarded her intently. 'You are saying that you do not care for Pietro?'

Suzanne heaved a sigh. 'Well, I care about him. Of course I care about him. I like him very much. But—but I don't love him, if that's what you mean.'

It struck her what a strange conversation this was to be having with a man she had only known for three days, but fortunately Elena was too young to appreciate the content of what they were saying.

Now Mazzaro leaned back, steepling his fingers, elbows resting on the polished arms of his chair. 'That is very interesting, Miss Hunt.'

'Why?' Suzanne forced herself to meet his gaze without flinching. 'People can be friends, *signore*. They don't always have to be—to be emotionally involved.'

'No, that is true. Although perhaps less true than you might imagine. However. . .' He moved his broad shoulders. 'My impression has been that Pietro does care about you.'

'He thinks he does,' Suzanne murmured, in a low tone, and Mazzaro's hands fell to rest on the arms of his chair.

'So. . .' His eyes moved over her expressive face. 'You would like to look at my collection, hmm?'

Suzanne nodded. 'If you don't mind. . .'

Mazzaro quirked a dark eyebrow. 'No, I do not mind,' he said levelly. 'But I do not think this morning is a good time to look at antiques. These days of heat are too pleasant to spend indoors, and the morning is the best time of all. Let us entertain you, Miss Hunt, Elena and I. Let us show you a little of our country, yes?'

Suzanne stared at him, then at Elena. The child was waiting for her reactions with evident interest, and while she showed no enthusiasm, she showed no opposition either.

'You, *signore*?' Suzanne at last managed faintly.

Mazzaro's eyes narrowed. 'You have some objection?'

Suzanne lifted her shoulders helplessly. 'Well— no, not exactly, but. . .'

'But what, Miss Hunt? Feel free to refuse, if you would rather.'

If she would rather! Suzanne drew in a trembling breath. It was not so much a question of what she would rather do, but what she *ought* to do. Mazzaro di Falcone was a threat, that much she understood, but she could hardly say that to him. And anything else could be interpreted in other ways. He might well assume it was his appearance which deterred her, when in fact she found him the most disturbing man she had ever met.

And there was Elena, watching her with those deep dark eyes. Hadn't she wanted a chance to spend time with the child, to talk to her, and make her laugh, to encourage her to shed that unnatural obedience which was making her its prisoner?

'If—if—you're sure you want to do this,' she stammered.

'I would not have suggested it otherwise,' he assured her dryly. 'What is wrong, Miss Hunt? Do you now find you care about Pietro's reactions to my invitation?'

'No!' Suzanne was very sure about that. She took a deep breath. 'I should like to go with you—and Elena, *signore*.'

'Good.' Getting up from his seat, Mazzaro stood freely for a moment before reaching for his sticks. Then, with a wry glance in her direction, he leaned on them as he made his way to the door. 'Finish your breakfast, Miss Hunt. I will have Luigi fetch the automobile from the garage.'

Elena had been stuffing the remains of her croissant into her mouth as he spoke, and now she gulped down the last of her orange juice and jumped up from her seat to follow him. But Mazzaro stopped in the doorway, stilling her bid for escape with a brief admonishment.

'Stay and keep Miss Hunt company in my absence, *piccola*,' he directed, gently but firmly. 'And speak English, do you understand?'

'*Si*, Papà.'

'English, Elena.'

'Yes, Papà.' Elena subsided into her seat again, and Mazzaro left them.

With more determination than hunger, Suzanne applied herself to the croissants Lucia had brought her, trying not to think about Pietro's attitude when he discovered what she planned to do. And he had every right to object, she admitted honestly to herself. Without his invitation, she would not be here. And what if his mother had changed her mind about going to Muvano?

Chewing thoughtfully, she encountered Elena's eyes upon her, and forced a smile. At least Pietro knew of her desire to be friendly with the child, and might not look for more subtle motivations.

'Do you go to school in Castelfalcone, Elena?' she asked, stirring sugar into her coffee, and not really expecting a reply.

'Do you like Papà, *signorina*?' Elena countered, and the unlooked-for challenge caused Suzanne to choke on her roll, and take several gulps of coffee before she was able to reply.

Her distress reacted on Elena as it would on any child. She giggled, hiding her mirth unsuccessfully behind her hand, unable to hide the laughter in her eyes.

'I—of course I like your *papà*,' Suzanne managed at last, and Elena sobered.

'Pietro does not,' she said candidly, her English almost as proficient as her father's. 'And you are his friend, are you not, *signorina*?'

'Just because Pietro and I are friends it does not mean that we always agree,' Suzanne said evenly. 'And in any case, I'm sure you're wrong. Pietro and your father are cousins. Cousins often have arguments, but they don't mean anything.'

Elena lifted her small shoulders. 'Mamma said that Pietro wanted to care for her; that is why he gets so angry with Papà.'

Suzanne stared at her aghast for a moment, and then poured herself some more coffee. 'You're too young to understand, Elena,' she said, without looking at the child. 'Now, tell me: do you go to school in Castelfalcone?'

'No.' Elena shook her head. 'I go to school in Milano.'

'Milano?' Suzanne echoed in surprise. 'Oh—you mean a boarding school.'

'It is a convent, *signorina*. When Papà—when Papà had his accident, Mamma said she could not cope with taking me to the school in Muvano. There is a convent there, too, you see, but the pupils must come home in the afternoon. So. . .' she made a continental little gesture, 'I went to Milano.'

It was distressingly easy for Suzanne to draw her own conclusions about the affair. Sophia had decided that Elena should go away to school, and Mazzaro's absence had given her the ideal opportunity and an excuse. Unless Mazzaro himself had suggested the change to give his wife more time to spend with him. . .

When Mazzaro returned, she had finished eating and was drinking a second cup of coffee.

'Are you ready?' he asked, standing by the doorway, his thighs lean and muscular in close-fitting corded pants. Looking at him, Suzanne could believe what Pietro had said about him. He did have sex appeal, and his injuries had in no way diminished that.

Elena jumped up and ran across to join her father, but Suzanne moved more slowly. 'I—is Pietro up?' she inquired evasively, but Mazzaro shook his head.

'Not yet. Why? Do you wish to gain his permission?'

The mockery in his tone rankled as he had no doubt intended that it should. 'I'm ready, *signore*,' she averred politely, and he smiled.

'I am glad. It is good to make an early start. Oh. . .' this as she moved away from the table, 'did you bring a swimsuit with you?'

'A swimsuit?' She was surprised. 'I—I think so, *signore*.'

'Then I should bring it with you, Miss Hunt,' he told her, drawing Elena aside from the door so that Suzanne could precede them into the hall. 'Do not concern yourself about towels. I have them in the car.'

Rather than argue with him, Suzanne went upstairs again, and retrieved the white bikini from the back of the drawer where Lucia had pushed it. She had packed it as an afterthought, not really expecting to need it, and its brevity made her wish she had denied its presence. But it was too late now, and she stuffed it into her denim bag along with her sunglasses and a tube of Ambre Solaire.

When she came down into the hall once more, sunlight was streaming through one of the long main doors, standing wide to the air. Dust motes floated in a shaft of brilliance that illuminated the mosaic tiles as she had never seen them before, and she halted uncertainly, wondering what was going on.

Then Mazzaro's stooped shadow darkened the doorway, and when he said: 'Come this way, Miss Hunt!' she walked slowly across the wide hall, passing him with a slight shiver to emerge into the sunlight at the front of the villa.

Shallow steps descended from the pillared portico to the sweep of gravel where a cream Mercedes was waiting, sleek and powerful, despite its evident age. The old man she and Pietro had encountered the evening they arrived was just flicking a duster over the bonnet, and she guessed he might be Luigi.

'Please—get into the automobile, Miss Hunt,' Mazzaro instructed, with that element of command in his voice which made her instinctively obey, and as she approached the vehicle, Luigi came round the back to open the nearside door for her. This morning the old man displayed none of the dourness he had exhibited with Pietro, and she could only assume that for some reason he did not like the younger man. Elena was already sitting in the back of the car, and the unusual animation of her features gave them an unexpected charm. She was more like her father than ever when she smiled, and Suzanne wished she would do it more often.

Mazzaro was coming down the steps now, and Suzanne looked away from the struggle he appeared to be having. But Luigi hurried to assist him, and presently he came slowly round the car, and levered himself and his sticks into the seat beside her. Luigi hesitated, concern showing in his gnarled face, but Mazzaro dismissed him firmly.

'I can manage, Luigi,' he assured him in his own language. 'Miss Hunt will see that I do not injure myself.'

The engine fired at the first attempt, and the huge coupé moved majestically down the drive. Looking about her at the metal struts supporting the hood,

Suzanne guessed it was of pre-war origin, but it had been cared for immaculately, and the leather upholstery was barely worn.

'Would you object to opening the gates for me, Miss Hunt?' Mazzaro requested as they approached the massive framework barring their way, and Suzanne shook her head quickly and jumped out of the car as soon as it stopped.

'Ought you to be driving?' she asked in an undertone, after the gates were closed again and they were descending the steep incline towards the village, and Mazzaro cast a faintly sardonic look in her direction.

'Nervous, Miss Hunt?' he queried mockingly, but she shook her head.

'No,' she denied. 'I—I just meant—'

'I know exactly what you meant,' he assured her gently, his mockery disappearing with astonishing swiftness. 'Let us say, there are members of my family who might consider my behaviour—reckless. But you and I—we know that is not so, do we not?'

Suzanne's breathing quickened. 'Do we?'

'Well, do we not?' He looked at her out of the corners of his eyes.

She wet her dry lips. 'If you say so, *signore*.'

He smiled. 'Do not be so tense, Miss Hunt. I promise you, you are quite safe in my hands.'

Suzanne wondered. Feeling safe was a mental as well as a physical condition. But watching his lean brown hands as they controlled the wheel, and experiencing the easy shifting of gears as they reached the foot of the hill, she knew that in the latter respect at least he was right.

They skirted the village, and passing through another of the arched gateways set in the crenellated walls, they began the descent into the valley. The windows of the car were open, and the scent of pine came strongly on the breeze, mingling with the damp smell of vegetation. Clumps of broom splashed the greenery with colour, and here and there, orchards of fruit trees displayed their own distinctive blossom.

Suzanne was enchanted, and sensing her interest, Mazzaro said laconically: 'Once the Falcone family owned the whole of this valley and the next, and so on as far as the Adriatic.'

Suzanne looked at him curiously. 'They must have been very rich.'

'And very powerful,' he conceded dryly. 'They were distantly related to the Medicis, and I understand they were amply rewarded for their butchery.'

'What a terrible thing to suggest!' she gasped, forgetting for a minute to whom she was speaking.

'But honest,' he insisted, smiling into her shocked eyes, and then she had to drag her gaze away from his, staring breathlessly out of the open windows, trying to control her uneven heartbeats. 'Italy has a savage history,' he went on, apparently noticing nothing amiss. 'It always makes me wonder how deep goes this veneer of civilisation we've succeeded in imposing upon our baser instincts.'

Suzanne tugged at a strand of sun-bleached hair. 'You—you think it's only a veneer? Civilisation, I mean?'

'Don't you?'

'I've never thought about it.'

'Perhaps you should. It might explain why after hundreds of years and dozens of wars, men still possess an almost pathological desire to kill and mutilate one another.'

Suzanne grimaced, chancing to look at him then. 'If that were true, surely there are other instincts equally dangerous!' she protested.

'There are,' he agreed softly. 'And as a beautiful woman, you must know I am right.'

Suzanne's colour deepened and she glanced over her shoulder apprehensively at Elena. But the child was absorbed in counting a flock of birds flying overhead, and when Suzanne looked back at Mazzaro, his amused expression made her realise he knew exactly what he was doing to her.

'I—I think you are teasing me, *signore*,' she told him stiffly, torturing the strap of her bag. 'I—where—where are we going?'

He shrugged lazily. 'Very well, Miss Hunt. If our conversation upsets you, we will change it.' He paused. 'Where am I taking you? Well perhaps we should ask Elena that question. Where are we going, *cara*?'

Elena's attention was arrested and she came to rest her bony little arms along the backs of their seats. '*A la cascata*, Papà?'

'*Si*, little one. To the waterfall. Have you ever swum in a waterfall, Miss Hunt?' His eyes mocked her. 'No, I am sure you have not. But today, with your permission, we will remedy that, *no*?'

Suzanne's palms were moist, and she could feel the heightening of emotion inside her as he looked at her. She tried to feel angry with him, and failed abysmally. How could she be angry with him when their time together was so fleeting, and every nerve in her body was responding to his lazy sexuality? She was glad that Elena was with them. Without the child's presence, the dangerous awareness she felt for her father might have been impossible to conceal.

They passed through a small village that bordered on the river, and then the track began to climb again through a thickly wooded area, studded with huge outcrops of rock. It was rough going in places, and once or twice Suzanne had to grab for the open window frame to prevent herself from being thrown against Mazzaro. But eventually they turned off the track between the trees, zigzagging down to a small clearing.

Before Mazzaro turned off the engine, they could hear the sounds of the waterfall. It was a wonderfully cooling sound, a gentle thunder, that echoed round the forest glade. There were other sounds, birds arguing in the trees over their heads and the rustle of small creatures in the undergrowth, but overall the rush of the water spread its musical resonance.

'Well? Shall we go and look?' Mazzaro suggested, and leant past her to push open her door. The action brought the hard length of his arm across her breasts, and although he didn't look at her, she sensed his awareness.

Then he thrust open his own door, and with a lithe movement swung his legs out and got to his feet. He pulled his seat forward so that Elena could climb out, too, and she showed no surprise at her father's apparent agility.

'Come along, Miss Hunt,' he said, as Suzanne still lingered in the car. 'It is not far.'

Reluctantly, Suzanne got out to face him, but to her relief, Elena had distracted his attention, asking whether she might go on ahead.

'Very well,' he was saying, 'but take care, *cara*. The rocks may be damp and slippery.'

'*Si*, Papà.'

With a delighted smile in his direction, Elena skipped away between the trees, making for the sound of the falls. Meanwhile, Mazzaro moved stiffly to the rear of the car, opening the boot and taking out a leather bag bulging with towels.

Suzanne watched anxiously. 'Ought you to be doing this?' she asked. 'I mean—do your doctors approve?'

Mazzaro came to stand looking down at her. 'My dear Miss Hunt, exercise is what I need. That is why I'm stiff.'

Suzanne bent her head. 'I see.'

'Your concern is touching,' he remarked dryly. 'An unknown commodity to me.' He lifted the denim bag off her shoulder. 'I'll carry that. Come, Elena will be wondering what we are doing.'

Suzanne looked up at him. 'She knows, doesn't she?'

'He nodded. 'It is our secret. A three-way secret now.'

'I'm sorry.' Suzanne moved her shoulders in a

dismissing gesture. 'If I hadn't wandered out on to my balcony. . .'

'. . .I shouldn't have had the pleasure of your company,' he finished softly. 'Or perhaps I should,' he added, his eyes moving to rest on her parted lips. 'Maybe there are some things I do not have to deny myself. . .'

CHAPTER FIVE

THE fall of water was perhaps twenty feet in height, flowing through a narrow opening which Mazzaro later explained was fed from an underground stream. There were many such channels, he added, pouring down from the mountains, ice-cold and clear as glass. The rock face behind the waterfall was covered in moss and ferns, but Suzanne could see how it might be possible to climb to the top. The water fell into a huge natural basin, about thirty feet across, before surging over its sides to tumble down the rock face to the river below. When Suzanne and Mazzaro emerged from the shadows of the trees, they were on a small plateau at the foot of the falls, where Elena was sitting, dangling her bare toes into the water.

Forgetting that since that moment at the car, she had not spoken to Mazzaro, Suzanne made an involuntary sound of pleasure. 'What a beautiful spot,' she exclaimed, looking about her in amazement. 'I've never seen such a place!'

'I am glad you like it.' Mazzaro came beside her, dropping his leather bag and her denim one down on to the grassy bank. 'As you can see, we can swim in the basin. It is very cold and deep, but there are no currents and it is quite safe.'

Suzanne glanced down at her bag. Even though he had suggested she bring her swimsuit, she had not intended to use it. But now she knew she could not resist the temptation to swim in this enchanted place.

Elena scrambled up. 'May I go in the water, Papà?' she asked, tugging at her long braids.

Mazzaro's expression was indulgent. 'Your swimsuit is in the bag,' he conceded lightly. 'You and Miss Hunt can go into the trees to change.'

'*Si*, Papà.'

Elena rummaged about in the leather bag and came out with a one-piece black swimsuit. Like the rest of her clothes, it was far too old for her, but all the same, Suzanne wished hers was similar. Elena's suit would make the bikini look even more daring.

She hesitated as the little girl waited for her, and Mazzaro bent and picked up her bag. 'You did bring a swimsuit, did you not, Miss Hunt?'

She nodded, reluctantly, taking the bag from his hand.

'Are you not going to swim?'

Suzanne bit her lip. 'Are you?'

Mazzaro began to unbutton his shirt. 'Does this answer your question, Miss Hunt?'

Suzanne turned away, and Elena gave her an appealing look. '*Avanti, signorina*,' she begged impatiently. '*Presto, per favore*!'

They went into the trees, and it took only a few moments for Suzanne to remove her slacks and vest and replace them with the pants and bra of the bikini. Elena had politely turned away while she was getting changed, but when she had put on her black swimsuit, she looked at Suzanne with admiring eyes.

'Zia Tommasa would not let me wear such a garment, *signorina*,' she said with a sigh. 'But you look very nice,' she added half apologetically.

Suzanne had to smile. 'Does Zia Tommasa choose all your clothes, Elena?' she asked, and the little girl nodded.

'Mamma does not have the time to go shopping with me,' she explained innocently, unwittingly revealing what little interest Sophia showed in her only offspring.

When Suzanne emerged from the trees behind Elena, she saw Mazzaro crouching on the rocks beside the pool. He was in brief black shorts that hung loosely on his hips, and she was able to admire the muscular expanse of his brown back. But the scars from his neck extended down over his shoulder blade, distorting the flesh in places, and her fingers itched to touch them.

He turned and straightened at their approach, showing Elena the tiny frog he had discovered in a rock pool. She scampered forward to examine it, and over her head, Mazzaro looked at Suzanne.

With anyone else, she would have known exactly what they were thinking, but Mazzaro's eyes were guarded, his expression enigmatic, as his eyes moved from her face, down the slender length of her body. Then, as Elena spoke to him, he looked away from Suzanne and down at his daughter, his features softening miraculously.

Suzanne would have liked to have examined the frog, too, but she felt *de* trop, and moving past them, she went to dip her toes into the icy water. Water from the cascade showered her bare shoulders, and she shivered in the spray, raising her face to its coolness.

The frog was apparently disposed of, and Elena came to join her at the pool's rim. 'It is very cold, *signorina*,' she said, raising her shoulders in a happy gesture of anticipation. Then, without hesitation, she dived headlong into the water, coming up a few yards away, spluttering with laughter.

Suzanne was astounded and she was hardly aware of Mazzaro coming to join her, until he said quietly: 'She swims like a fish, does she not?'

'Yes, she does.' Suzanne's eyes darted nervously at him. 'She seems to love the water.'

'She does.' A smile lifted the corners of his mouth. 'Do you? Or is this outfit more for decoration than participation?'

Suzanne's hands moved automatically to cover herself. 'I don't have anything else, *signore*,' she said, noticing that there were scars on his collarbone, too. Afraid that he might think she was staring, she looked away again, adding quickly: 'I didn't expect to need a swimsuit.'

He sighed then, bending to rinse his hands in the icy water. As he straightened, he looked up at her and she was forced to meet his gaze.

'Why don't you look at me?' he asked softly. 'What are you afraid of? I don't mind.'

'Don't you?'

'Not if you don't,' he answered, watching her.

She let her eyes wander away from the scars, across the width of his chest and down to his navel.

'Will you tell me about your accident?' she asked daringly, and his hand came out and lifted her chin.

'Not now,' he said huskily.

'But later?'

'If you want me to.'

If she wanted him to! Dizziness assailed her as she looked up into his lean dark face. His eyes were green pools in which she would have willingly drowned herself. Wanton desires surfaced, encouraging her to move closer to him, needing to feel the hardness of his flesh against hers. She could smell the warm heat of his body, and her hands came up as if she would touch him. Then, with an agonised exclamation, she dragged herself away. Was she going quite mad? Just because he had been kind to her, spoken to her on equal terms, she was imagining all manner of foolish things, allowing her own stupid emotions to get in the way of common sense.

'If—if the water's—as—as cold as Elena—' she was stammering incoherently, when his hand on her nape silenced her.

'Be still,' he said insistently, bending his head until his lips brushed her hair. He was standing behind her, and to Elena's uninformed gaze their positions looked perfectly innocent.

'I'm—sorry,' she muttered foolishly, and he uttered an angry imprecation under his breath.

'Why are you sorry?' he demanded, his fingers moving until they spread possessively across her throat. 'Do you think I don't want to touch you?'

She took an involuntary step backward and came up against the solid weight of his body. 'This is crazy,' she breathed and then caught her breath when his hand slid down her shoulder to her bare midriff, moving on over her hip to rest for a devastating minute against her thigh.

Then he propelled her away from him again, gently but firmly, and without another word, walked past her to dive into the pool as his daughter had done. He swam underwater for some distance, coming up beside Elena, within the cascade of the waterfall, letting her duck him and making her squeal with laughter when he threw water over her.

Watching them, Suzanne felt the coldness of reality creeping over her again. Oh God, she thought sickly, realising what she had done. What must he really be thinking of her? Throwing herself at him like that, letting him touch her in a wholly intimate way. He probably thought she was easy game for any man. And that simply was not true! She just had no control over her emotions where he was concerned.

Mazzaro eventually left Elena again to swim back to the side. 'Are you coming in?' he asked, and she noticed he did not say 'Miss Hunt' as he had done before.

'I don't know,' she answered stiffly. 'I don't want to intrude.'

'Intrude? *Dio mio!*' he swore softly, pulling himself up out of the water. 'You are not intruding, Suzanne. There—I have said your name. I cannot go on calling you Miss Hunt. You don't mind?'

'Would it matter if I did?' she asked tightly, and he stared impatiently at her.

'What is it? What's the matter?' His eyes darkened as he got to his feet. 'You are angry with me for what happened before.'

'I'm angry with myself,' she corrected him.

'Why?'

'Why?' She gazed at him. 'I am not—not a girl like that, *signore*. I haven't—I have never—' She broke off frustratedly. 'Oh, you know what I'm trying to say.'

'I know you are being foolish,' he said flatly. 'And you know my name, if you would care to use it.'

'I can't call you by your Christian name!' she protested.

'Why not? Don't you like it? I have two others if they would suit you better—'

'Oh, please. . .' She turned away from him. 'Stop it!'

'Then stop making what you English call mountains out of molehills. What did we do that was so wrong? You are a beautiful girl, Suzanne. You don't need me to tell you that. But if by touching you I have offended you, I am sorry. Whatever you think, I did not intend any insult. Nor do I consider you any differently now than before.'

She half turned towards him. 'But if Elena had not been here—'

His eyes narrowed. 'Yes. Well, she is here. And I came to my senses, hmm?'

'But *I* didn't!' she cried.

'And that has never happened to you before?'

'No!'

'Not even with Pietro?'

'Pietro? No! I've told you, we don't have that kind of relationship!'

'You surprise me—'

'Why?' She stared angrily at him. 'You must have a very low opinion of the morals of English girls!'

'I would not confine my impressions to English girls—'

'Oh, thanks! But there are other things in life, you know!'

He considered her frustrated features. 'You are saying you have never—slept with a man?'

'Yes. *Yes!*' she seethed. 'Just because you find it easy to seduce a woman, don't imagine all your sex are as successfull!'

He shifted impatiently then, his bare feet digging into the soft earth. 'What justification do you have for saying that to me?' he demanded quietly. 'It would seem that you, too, have acquired a faulty impression of me, Suzanne.'

She heaved a sigh. 'Then perhaps we'd better leave it,' she said, turning away. 'It's a ridiculous conversation anyway.'

'Is it?' He was not prepared to let her go yet. 'Why? Because you know there are few women who would welcome my attentions?'

'That's nonsense, and you know it,' she flared, swinging round on him again, forgetting who he was in the heat of the moment. 'You're a very attractive man!'

'You think so?' he probed, and she moved her head in a helpless gesture.

'You know I do.'

'Thank you.' A faint smile touched his lips. 'And now, I think, we will join Elena, *no*?'

Suzanne was glad to give in and get into the water. It was marvellous to feel its coldness melting away her anger and frustration, to swim under the torrent of water and feel its pressure easing away her doubts and anxieties. She was content right now to live for the moment, and she refused to think beyond the next few hours.

Mazzaro retrieved a plastic ball from the car, and for a while they played a kind of water polo that involved much splashing and laughter, with Mazzaro competing against the two girls and cheating unashamedly. There were times when he and Suzanne swam to reach the ball simultaneously, and during their struggles she often felt his legs against hers, and once she grabbed his shoulders in her excitement and felt the ridges of his scars beneath her hands.

At last they were all exhausted, and pulled themselves out on to the grassy plateau to rest. Mazzaro stretched his length lazily, and Elena flung herself on top of him, indulging in a playful wrestling match until he protested that she had defeated him. Suzanne was selfconscious out of the water again, and sat with her legs drawn up, her arms wrapped around them, her chin resting on her knees. The sun beat down on her bare back, but she didn't notice it, intent as she was on avoiding Mazzaro's eyes.

Elena eventually wandered off to pick wild flowers, and Suzanne started when Mazzaro got up, too. He walked up the bank, and when she chanced a glance at him over her shoulder, she saw him pulling a towel out of the leather bag. He came back again, drying his chest and shoulders, and halted beside Suzanne.

'You will get burned, if you are not careful,' he said, looking down at her, and she shrugged her shoulders.

'I don't think so.'

'I do.' He came down on his haunches beside her. 'Would you like me to dry your back?'

'No!' Her eyes were wide with alarm. 'I can do it.'

He inclined his head. 'I'll get you a towel. . .'

'I can get one.' She rose quickly to her feet, finding herself in the position of being able to look down on him for the first time in their association. 'In the bag?'

He nodded, and with a resigned pressure of his lips, subsided on to the turf again, drying his arms and legs with a rather pensive air.

Suzanne took out a thick red towel, and quickly wrapped her slim body in its folds. It enveloped her like a toga, and she rubbed vigorously at her hair with one end. Mazzaro finished drying himself, and rolled on to his stomach. Then folding his arms beneath his chin, he watched her.

'How did you come to meet Pietro?' he asked suddenly, and Suzanne lifted her head to look at him.

'Why do you want to know?'

'Pietro has had girls before. They were not like you.'

'You mean—he has brought other girls to the Villa Falcone?'

Mazzaro inclined his head. 'It is his home, after all.'

Suzanne shrugged. 'I didn't think of it, somehow. I suppose his mother—I mean—'

She broke off awkwardly, and he smiled. 'Zia Tommasa can be quite intimidating, I agree.'

'I wasn't about to say that,' she retorted crossly.

'Then what?'

'I don't know now.' She turned too quickly and stepped on a corner of the towel and it fell to the ground. Her first instincts were to snatch it up again, but that would have been too obvious, so she knelt down beside her own bag and extracted the tube of sun-tan cream. Unscrewing the cap, she applied some to her arms and massaged determinedly, trying not to think about him watching her.

'So. . .' he prompted. 'How did you meet Pietro?'

Suzanne sighed. 'It was in an antique shop, actually. He was trying to find the price of this article, and the assistant didn't understand him. As I spoke Italian, naturally I offered to help.'

'I see.' Mazzaro pushed his lower lip upward in a thoughtful grimace. 'That explains it. But I'm surprised that you, with your inhibitions, should allow yourself to become involved with a stranger like that!'

It took a few moments for her to realise he was teasing her again, and when she did, a reluctant smile curved her lips. They smiled at each other quite openly for a few seconds, and then, without warning, that involuntary awareness stirred between them again, darkening his eyes, and causing her to look quickly away from him.

Breathing shallowly, she almost jumped out of her skin when his arm brushed against hers as he took the tube of Ambre Solaire from her unresisting fingers. Kneeling beside her, he applied a worm-like measure of the cream to his palm, and then spread it smoothly over her back and the nape of her neck. He didn't speak, nor did she, but his hands were frankly caressing.

Then Elena came dancing back to them, her arms full of her gatherings, tiny wild daisies and meadow-wort, mixed up with milkmaid and weeds of all kinds. With a groan, Mazzaro rolled away from Suzanne to lie prone upon the grass, his face hidden in its coolness.

'Is something wrong with Papà?' Elena asked worriedly, reverting to Italian in her distress, but Suzanne quickly reassured her, screwing the cap back on to the sun-tan cream, busying herself by putting it away in her bag.

'What have you found?' she added, and Elena forgot her anxieties in displaying her bounty.

'Perhaps you could take them home and find out all their names,' Suzanne suggested, smoothing the petals of a pansy. 'Then you could start a collection.'

Elena looked doubtful. 'Zia Tommasa would not let me take wild flowers into the Villa, *signorina*,' she said, shaking her head.

Suzanne sighed impatiently, and then on impulse, she leant across and stroked Mazzaro's leg just above the joint of his knee. He flinched away from her

touch, and she hastened quickly into speech, hardly
aware that she used his name until his eyes encountered hers in frank appraisal.

'Mazzaro, couldn't Elena take her flowers back to
the villa? She—she says your aunt might object.'

Mazzaro's expression was enigmatic. 'And do you
think she should be allowed to take them back,
Suzanne?' he asked, deliberately involving her in the
decision, and she nodded quickly. 'All right.' He
nodded at Elena. 'If Zia Tommasa has any complaint,
you can refer her to me.'

'Oh, thank you, Papà!' Elena dropped the plants
she was holding to fling her arms around his neck,
but over the child's shoulder it was Suzanne who
felt the disturbing consideration of his regard.

They left the falls some thirty minutes later,
Suzanne having put on her slacks over her bikini,
leaving the vest in her bag. Sitting beside Mazzaro
in the car she was very much aware of the dramatic
change in their relationship, but she doubted it meant
as much to him as it did to her. Nevertheless, he was
more serious than on the journey out, and seemed to
be concentrating exclusively on his driving.

They stopped for coffee in the village they had
passed on their way to the falls. It was almost noon,
and the small *piazza* was thronged with people, many
of whom knew and recognised Mazzaro. Several of
the men stopped to have a word with him as he and
Suzanne and Elena were seated outside one of the
pavement cafés, and they cast curious glances in
Suzanne's direction, clearly wondering who his companion might be. But Mazzaro did not introduce her,

and only Elena came in for some smiling admiration of the armful of flowers she had insisted on carrying with her.

It was almost one o'clock when they arrived back at the villa. Luigi was there to open the gates for them this time, and he doffed his cap politely as Mazzaro drove through. They drove straight to the stables and garage block, as Pietro had done the evening he and Suzanne had arrived, and Elena heaved a sigh of regret as her father dragged his sticks from the back of the car.

'Papà. . .' she began, but his expression daunted her, and she got out of the car after him without another word.

Suzanne draped the strap of her bag over her shoulder as Mazzaro closed the car door and assumed his usual stooped position. 'I—well, thank you,' she said awkwardly, as he began to move towards the house and she fell into step beside him. 'I—I've enjoyed myself.'

'Have you?' He glanced her way. 'I am glad.'

His tone was more stiff than she had heard before, and her lips parted anxiously. 'Is something wrong?' she exclaimed, glad that Elena was some way ahead of them. 'Are you in pain?'

The sound he made was scornful. 'That depends what kind of pain you are talking about,' he said flatly. 'No, Suzanne, I am not in pain. And forgive me if I have upset you at all. That was not my intention.'

'You haven't upset me,' she protested, but his lips twisted contemptuously.

'I doubt if Pietro would agree with you,' he commented dourly, and with this strange remark, he kept silent until they entered the villa.

Pietro himself met them in the hall, and it was obvious to anyone that he was not in the best of tempers.

'Where the hell have you been?' he demanded in his own language, his tone harsh and angry. His eyes shifted to Mazzaro just behind her. 'I might have known you were at the bottom of it!'

'Please, Pietro. . .' Suzanne glanced meaningfully at Elena who was just in front of her, her head tilted in surprise to look at her father's cousin. 'There's no need to shout. I—we—all of us have been to see some falls—'

'Have you?' Pietro interrupted her fiercely. 'How nice for you! But of course, it did not occur to you to tell me where you were going, did it?'

'That is enough, Pietro,' stated Mazzaro, speaking for the first time. 'Miss Hunt is not answerable to you for her whereabouts. It was understood that you were taking your mother to Muvano—'

'That's true. I did take Mamma to Muvano, but—' Pietro said a word that made Mazzaro's hands tighten on the sticks, 'I was back in an hour. Did you expect me to stay in Muvano, gossiping like an old woman?'

Mazzaro's mouth curled. 'That was my estimate of the situation,' he retorted, with deliberate provocation, and Pietro took a menacing step towards him; although what he thought he could do against the older man. Suzanne could not imagine.

'Please. . .' she intervened, afraid of the grimness

in Mazzaro's expression. 'Pietro, I'm sorry if you've wasted time, hanging about for me. But I honestly thought you would be away all morning.' She sighed. 'Didn't Lucia tell you where I'd gone?'

'Lucia!' Pietro almost spat the word. 'Don't you know the servants around here only answer to their lord and master?' he sneered. '*He* has them well trained not to reveal his whereabouts. I wonder why?'

Elena, whose troubled eyes had been going from one to another of them, pursed her lips in dismay and burst into tears. 'You're being horrid, Pietro!' she sobbed, shreds of the blossom she was clutching tumbling unheeded to the marble floor. 'We've had a lovely morning, and now you're spoiling everything! Just because Papà likes Suzanne, you're jealous! *Jealous!* Papà doesn't get angry when you entertain Mamma. And he could, couldn't he? Because I've seen you kissing her. I have. I have! Only Mamma said not to say anything, because it would only cause trouble! It would have served you right if Papà had kissed Suzanne, but he didn't. I wished he *would!*'

CHAPTER SIX

MAZZARO did not join them for lunch, and as Signora Vitale was still at Muvano, there was only Suzanne, Pietro and Elena at the table. Sophia's whereabouts had not been mentioned, but Suzanne was rapidly gathering that the Contessa led her own life apart from the family.

The atmosphere was tense to say the least. Elena, after that outburst in the hall, had rushed away to her own room, and Suzanne had been relieved to do the same. She needed to change, she had said, which was true, but more than that she needed time alone to reorganise her thoughts.

But had they been reorganised? she wondered, spooning chilled soup into her mouth without really tasting it. Her feelings for Mazzaro were just as mixed up as before, and her assessment of the situation at the villa was deteriorating hourly. It was obvious that the relationships between these people were not the simple ones they might appear, and she wondered whether Sophia's involvement with Pietro had had anything to do with the apparent breakdown of her marriage. The trouble was, she was emotionally inclined to blame Sophia for everything, when in fact Mazzaro was equally as possible a suspect. That moment by the waterfall, for example, had not been entirely one-sided, and there might be other entanglements which as yet she did not know about. Yet she couldn't altogether believe that. It wasn't only her emotions that convinced her that Mazzaro di Falcone was an honourable man.

Elena, for her part, was more subdued than usual. For once, Suzanne could have wished for Signora Vitale's presence. She, at least, was not involved in all this, and her astringency was what was needed to heal the breach between them. As it was, Pietro was silent and morose, and Suzanne had great difficulty in drawing more than a fleeting smile from Elena.

When Lucia had served the coffee, Elena excused herself, and although for one awful moment Suzanne thought that Pietro was going to say something unpleasant to the child, he let her go, and the door closed behind her. But then they were alone, and in some ways that was worse.

Feeling obliged to make at least an attempt to restore a sense of normality between them, Suzanne poured his coffee, adding the cream and sugar she knew he liked, and pushed it across to him.

'Thank you.'

He was polite, and she felt relief flooding through her. But it was almost immediately replaced by contempt for her own duplicity, and shaking her head, she said: 'I think I ought to go home,' in a low tone.

Pietro's head jerked up. 'What did you say?'

'I think you heard, Pietro. Would you telephone the airport for me? Find out if there are any flights to London this evening or tomorrow that I could take.'

'No.' Pietro made a frustrated sound. 'Suzanne, you can't leave!'

'On the contrary, I think my being here is just—causing trouble,' she said evenly.

'What do you mean?' Pietro stared at her, and she wondered if he suspected she had said more than she intended. Then he shook his head. 'If you mean that business with Mazzaro, forget it! He and I have never—liked one another.' To her surprise, he coloured. 'As for what Elena said about Sophia—well, I'm not denying that I—that she—well, that we are very fond of one another. Elena saw us kissing. I don't deny that, but—'

'Oh, listen, Pietro!' she cried desperately. 'You don't have to justify yourselves to me! It's nothing to do with me!'

'That's not true, Suzanne. I don't want you to get the wrong impression about me—'

'Pietro, my impression of you hasn't changed.' But was that strictly true? Too late now to retract the words anyway. 'And I told you before I came out here—we're just friends, that's all. Friends! Stop trying to pretend a relationship between us that simply doesn't exist.'

'How can I pretend what I know is true, for me at least?' he protested, spreading his arms in a dramatic gesture.

'Suzanne, the more time I spend with you, the more I know that I was right to ask you here. And Mamma is beginning to like you, too. Please, don't disappoint us both by running away from the first little obstacle!'

'The first little obstacle?' Suzanne gave a confused shrug. 'The first obstacle to what, Pietro? I've already explained how I feel. I'm sorry if you think you care for me, but surely that is just another reason for me to leave!'

'Suzanne! Suzanne! All right, I admit, I was rude this morning, but try and see my point of view—'

'I do see your point of view, Pietro.'

'—I was furious when I knew you had gone out with Mazzaro. I know the kind of man he is. I knew you would hear nothing good of me from him.'

'That's not true, Pietro. Mazzaro—' She broke off as his name slipped too easily from her lips. 'I mean—your cousin said nothing derogatory about you, believe me.'

Pietro's nostrils flared. 'I suppose he's too clever for that! Of course, I should have guessed. He has more subtle ways of putting me down. Like making sure I'd be around when you got back.'

'Oh, Pietro!' Suzanne sighed. 'You're being hysterical! Like I said, I'd like to leave—'

'I won't let you go. You came here for the weekend. How do you think I'll feel if you clear off on Saturday? Mamma will wonder what has gone wrong. She'll be sure to suspect—'

Now he broke off, and Suzanne suddenly knew what he had been about to say. Signora Vitale, with her attitudes, would never condone a relationship between her son and Sophia. What if she suspected them already? If she, Suzanne, left unexpectedly, there were bound to be questions that Pietro would find very hard to answer.

Tracing the rim of her coffee cup with her finger, Suzanne spoke quietly. 'If I choose to leave, Pietro, you can't stop me.'

He hunched his shoulders then, and resting his elbows on the table, he supported his chin in his hands. 'You suspect, don't you? About Sophia and me? You believe Elena.'

'Do you think I care?' Impatiently, Suzanne pushed her chair away from the table and got to her feet. 'No. It just seems to me that my being here is acting as a catalyst on you all. I—none of this has anything to do with me. It's a family affair.'

'Yes, it is.' His arms fell to rest on the table. 'All right, so I can't force you to stay. Don't you think you owe me something for inviting you here? The least you can do, as far as I can see, is stay for the agreed period.'

Suzanne, who had been standing by the long serving table, smoothing the palms of her hands against its cool polished surface, now turned to face him resignedly. The things he had said, the persuasions he had made, this of all of them made sense. And what was more, there was no argument against it.

'Oh, Pietro!' she exclaimed, and he seized on her weakening.

'You agree?'

She shook her head. 'I don't agree.' She sighed. 'But I know you're right. All right, Pietro, I'll stay until Tuesday, as planned.'

A smile removed the petulance from his expression. 'You won't regret it. And I promise, I won't do anything else to upset you.'

'To upset me?' Suzanne's echo of his words was ironic. *Let me not do anything to upset you*! she thought uneasily. There was a guest for dinner that evening.

Signora Vitale had returned from Muvano. Suzanne had gone with Pietro to fetch his mother home, and she had enjoyed the brief outing. Away from the Villa, Pietro was a much nicer person, much more like the man she had first got to know.

But the guest was male; young and attractive, and obviously wealthy, judging by the cut of his clothes and the heavy gold bracelet and rings he wore. He came into the salon with Sophia, and from the way she was clinging to his arm, they seemed to be more than just good friends. Suzanne's eyes went straight to Mazzaro, who was standing before the sculpted marble fireplace, but his face was expressionless as he leaned there on his sticks, and when Sophia's escort came to greet him, he was coolly indifferent to their intimacy. In a black mohair dinner jacket, he was a disturbing Machiavelli, in Suzanne's opinion, a far more devastating personality than the newcomer, Carlo Bottega.

Suzanne herself had dressed for dinner with rather more care than usual. She had not known they were to have a guest, but it did something for her morale to know that she was looking her best. Her halter-necked gown of black silk, clung in all the right places, and accentuated the extreme fairness of her hair. Certainly Carlo Bottega seemed to think so, and Sophia became quite impatient with him when he showed his evident admiration for the younger girl.

Pietro, too, seemed unable to take his eyes off her, and not even Sophia's appearance with the other man had been enough to disconcert him.

Only Mazzaro avoided speaking to her. He had acknowledged her presence with a brief nod, but if he found her appearance pleasing he did not say so. On the contrary, if she had not known better, Suzanne would have said that he did not like her very much, and the chilling thought that perhaps he regretted his behaviour that morning, would not be displaced. It made her turn more eagerly to Carlo Bottega's obvious attractions, basking in the warmth of admiration uncooled by frozen green eyes.

Afterwards, she didn't remember what they ate, only that Pietro's mother had spent the whole meal distracting Sophia's attention, leaving Carlo free to talk to Suzanne. Pietro was no more suited by this arrangement than his cousin's wife, but Signora Vitale was the kind of woman who would not easily be diverted. Suzanne suspected that her interference was deliberate—that she disliked Sophia's involvement with the attractive young Italian just as much as her association with her own son. Was it Mazzaro's marriage she was trying to preserve? Suzanne wondered why that conclusion filled her with such unease.

When dinner was over, Sophia attempted to draw Carlo out into the gardens through the long french windows opening from the small salon. But he was annoyingly obtuse, and she stood aside impatiently as he drank his coffee with Suzanne.

'I am often in London,' he was saying, much to

the younger girl's embarrassment. 'I have business associations there. My company specialises in Italian marble, and there is an increasing market for that kind of thing. We have been fortunate enough to— what would you say?—commercialise our product? You would be surprised how many people still want sun-terraces, and patios, and swimming pools in these inflationary times.'

Suzanne endeavoured to sound interested. 'I suppose so.'

'Naturally, I do not work all the time I am in London,' Carlo went on, seemingly oblivious to Sophia's simmering anger. 'I enjoy the theatre, and I always try to see some new show while I am there.' He gave her a conspiratorial smile. 'It is amazing how simple it is to get tickets if one has the right connections.'

'I'm sure.'

'Do you work in London, Miss Hunt?'

Suzanne was about to reply when the sound of Mazzaro's sticks approaching them across the floor stilled her vocal cords. Only Sophia seemed to welcome his interruption, for it was obvious from the expression on his face that he did not approve of their isolation from the other members of the party.

'My aunt has some embroidery she wishes you to see, Miss Hunt,' he said unsmilingly. 'Sophia, I thought you intended to show our guest my latest creation.'

'So I did, Mazzaro.' Sophia straightened from her petulant slouch. 'But Miss Hunt has been showing an unusual interest in Carlo's occupation.'

Suzanne refused to answer such an outrageous suggestion. With a faintly apologetic smile in Carlo's direction, she moved away across the salon to where Signora Vitale was seated, handling a frame of exquisitely worked tapestry. Pietro was standing beside his mother, and he slipped a proprietorial arm around Suzanne's waist as he indicated the minute stitching that made up the peacock design of the panel.

'Wall hangings, such as this, were very popular in the fifteenth and sixteenth centuries,' commented Signora Vitale, fingering the mellowing colours with reverence. 'But here—see?—it is wearing away, and soon, left unattended, a hole would appear. You can imagine what a tragedy that would be.'

'Mamma repairs the tapestries,' explained Pietro proudly. 'Look, she has already made some stitches here. They are practically impossible to see.'

'You're very talented, signora,' murmured Suzanne politely, appreciating the older woman's skill, but ever conscious of her nephew who had come to join them. 'I'm sure I could never sew with such fine thread.'

'One never knows what one can do until one tries,' Mazzaro commented behind her. 'But she is right, Zia Tommasa, you are skilful at your task. And I am grateful for the time you expend.'

'Preserving your collection, Mazzaro?' Pietro taunted maliciously, but his cousin refused to be drawn.

'Where have Sophia and that young libertine gone?' asked Signora Vitale, ignoring her son, and

Mazzaro shifted so that Suzanne could see his face; and he could see hers.

'They have gone to the greenhouses, Zia Tommasa,' he replied smoothly. 'To see the roses.'

'The roses!' his aunt echoed, curling her lip.

'Yes, Zia Tommasa, the roses.' He looked deliberately at Suzanne. 'You must see my roses before you leave, Miss Hunt. I believe I have some particularly fine specimens.'

Before Suzanne could reply, Pietro's hand dropped from her waits. 'Another collection?' he sneered.

'What is the new rose called, Mazzaro?' Again Signora Vitale intervened.

'The Medici White,' he answered, and Suzanne recalled that delicately coloured blossom she had found lying on her breakfast tray. As if aware of what she was thinking, he looked at her again. 'You must see it, Miss Hunt. Magnolia white, like the skin of Catherine de Medici herself, and tinged with blood, as all the Medicis were at one time or another.'

Suzanne refused to meet his gaze. 'I'm afraid one rose is much like another to me, *signore*,' she said, earning Pietro's approval, but not for one moment did she think that Mazzaro believed her.

Signora Vitale's hands were restless on the embroidery frame. Obviously, Sophia's disappearance concerned her more than the merits of rose growing. 'And you really think Sophia is interested in horticulture?' she muttered, half to herself. 'Mazzaro, you are a fool!'

It was unlike Signora Vitale to forget herself, and as soon as the words were spoken, Suzanne could sense her regret. But Mazzaro merely moved his shoulders in a dismissing gesture, and said: 'Better a fool than a thief, Zia Tommasa,' and limped heavily away.

It was late when Sophia and her escort eventually returned to the salon. Suzanne was sitting with Signora Vitale, listening to her relating tales about the time before the war when she was a girl, living at the Villa Falcone. When she came to the instance of her own marriage, she glossed over the details hastily, leaving Suzanne in little doubt that her marriage to Bernardo Vitale had been frowned upon by her own family. He had not been a wealthy man, and probably even then the Falcones had been praying for a rich son-in-law to restore the family fortunes. Although Signora Vitale did not say so, it appeared that she had not been welcome in the Villa until Mazzaro's father was dead.

Mazzaro, who had left them earlier on, had not returned to join them, and although Suzanne was not vastly interested in Signora Vitale's reminiscences, they were preferable to Pietro's repeated suggestions to walk in the gardens. She had agreed to stay on at the Villa, it was true, but that was all. She wanted no awkward involvements with anyone.

Sophia looked a little disappointed that Mazzaro was not there to witness her return. That Carlo Bottega had been kissing her was obvious from the bare state of her full mouth, and she moved languidly, as if conscious of her power over the younger man.

Suzanne waited only the few moments that politeness decreed before excusing herself. Both Pietro and

Carlo Bottega expressed their regret that she was leaving them, but the sanctuary of her room was what Suzanne craved most. She hurried along the gallery to the main hall, and was about to mount the staircase when the awareness that she was not alone made her glance apprehensively over her shoulder.

Mazzaro was standing beneath the sculpted entrance to the unused wing of the Villa, a shadowy figure watching her. She paused, one hand on the balustrade, her foot on the lowest tread of the staircase, not quite knowing whether to acknowledge his presence or not.

Then he moved slightly forward, with the aid of his sticks, and said quietly: 'You retire early, Suzanne.'

She moistened her lips. 'It's after eleven, *signore*.' Impossible to say Mazzaro, even though they were alone.

'Is it? Is it really?' Mazzaro's tone was dry. 'But surely that is early for a girl like you?'

Suzanne stepped down on to the marble tiles of the hall, needing to feel a firm foundation beneath her feet. 'Is it, *signore*?'

Mazzaro took another step forward. 'Young women these days—need to live life to the full, do they not?'

Suzanne frowned. 'To the full, *signore*?' She was repeating his words, but she couldn't help herself.

'Of course.' Another dragging of his feet. Why did he persist in doing it? She wondered half frustratedly. 'They feel the need to experience all aspects of human behaviour, no?'

There was more to his conversation than the surface urbanity he was maintaining. Suzanne felt the first twinges of dismay. 'I don't think I understand you, *signore*—' she was beginning, when he interrupted her, covering the space between them with disconcerting speed.

'That man, *signorina*—Carlo Bottega. My wife's—pretty boy. You find him attractive, do you not?'

Suzanne drew a trembling breath. 'I—he's an attractive man, *signore*,' she stammered. 'I—I'm sorry about—'

'Spare me the platitudes, *signorina*, please. I am not quite the fool my aunt gives me credit for being.'

'You—you're not a fool at all!' she protested.

'No?' Dark brows descended over eyes narrowed to slits in the shadowy illumination emanating from bronze lamps behind him. '*Signorina*, I heard Bottega making an assignation with you. I advise you not to accept.'

Suzanne gasped. 'I beg your pardon!'

Mazzaro's nostrils flared. 'Please do not attempt to deny it, *signorina*. My hearing is very acute. I regret if I am embarrassing you, but I do not wish that you should interfere with my plans.'

Any momentary flicker of excitement that he should behave as if he was jealous of Carlo Bottega revealing an interest in her was as quickly extinguished. Where before her legs had felt weak, now her whole body stiffened with humiliation.

Holding her head up high, she stated coldly: 'Obviously your hearing is too acute for me, *signore*. I regret, I missed hearing Signor Bottega's invitation.

Perhaps I should return to the salon and ask him to repeat it.'

Mazzaro's mouth hardened. 'You deny he invited you to attend the theatre with him?'

Suzanne shivered at the look in his eyes, but her voice was cold with anger as she said: 'I neither admit nor deny anything. I don't consider that you have any right at all to ask me such questions.'

'So long as you are a guest under my roof, *signorina*, I hold myself responsible for your welfare—'

'Does that include my moral welfare, *signore*?'

'For a young woman who only this morning was professing her innocence, *signorina*, you are remarkably aggressive in defence of your—independence.'

Suzanne stared at him mutely, her lips moving helplessly, and then, unable to think of any suitable retort, she turned once more to the stairs, mounting several before his voice halted her again.

'You wished to see my collection, *signorina*,' he said, in a coolly detached tone, and she swung round, wishing she dared tell him what he could do with his precious collection right at this moment. 'If you would care to join me for breakfast in the morning, I will conduct you round the Villa myself.'

'Thank you, but I am going to Mass with Pietro and his mother in the morning,' she retorted ungraciously. Then, on impulse: 'Will you be there?'

'I regret, my connections with the church were severed some time ago, *signorina*. About the same time that I learned that there are more gods to worship than churches built to them.'

Suzanne took an involuntary step down the stairs again. 'I'm afraid I don't understand you, *signore*.'

Mazzaro's lips twisted. 'Wasn't it your writer, Jonathan Swift, who said: *We have just enough religion to make us hate, but not enough to make us love one another*—no?'

'Has your—did your accident—'

'—open my eyes, *signorina*?'

'That was not what I was about to say.'

'I'm sorry. Please—go ahead.'

His sardonic tone almost made her draw back again. But she remained where she was, holding tightly to the wrought iron baluster. 'I don't think bitterness solves anything, *signore*.'

'Bitterness?' His laugh was short and mirthless. 'My dear Suzanne, I am not bitter about the accident. Disillusioned, perhaps; regretful, definitely. But bitter, no. My—accident is something I look on with gratitude.' His eyes challenged hers mockingly. 'That surprises you? It should not. Where once I was blind, now I can see.'

Suzanne was tired, more tired than she had realised. His words didn't make sense. Only a garbled kind of awareness of what he was trying to say penetrated the throbbing that had started behind her temples.

'If—if you will excuse me, *signore*,' she murmured. 'I—I have a headache. . .'

Mazzaro's mockery disappeared. 'My apologies, *signorina*,' he said, bowing his head in dismissal. 'Of course I will not detain you any longer. Goodnight.'

Suzanne remained hesitatingly where she was as

he went back towards the archway where she had
first seen him. Contrarily, now she wished she had
not said what she had. It was not a headache that
was making her temples throb, but the awareness of
her own unwilling involvement with this man. She
wished she could go after him and comfort him, show
him that all women were not the same. But even that
was outrageous presumption. Why should he need
comforting? He was obviously very much in control
of the situation, in spite of Sophia's shortcomings,
and his attitude did not encourage sympathy.

Yet for all that, that was what she felt for him.
That, and an attraction which made her glad she was
returning to London in two days' time.

CHAPTER SEVEN

THE following day, Suzanne did not see Mazzaro at all.

In the morning she attended the small church of San Lorenzo with Pietro, his mother and Elena, and although she enjoyed the simple service, her thoughts constantly strayed to Mazzaro, and what he might be doing. To say she regretted not accepting his offer to show her his collection seemed a mild statement of her emotions.

During the afternoon, she sunbathed on her balcony while Signora Vitale and Elena rested, refusing Pietro's suggestion that they drove the sixty or so kilometres to the beach. She did not doubt that they would get there. It was the journey back to the Villa which troubled her. Since the day before, their relationship had changed somehow, and maybe the knowledge that all was not well between them had made him reckless.

She encountered Elena on the loggia as the shadows were lengthening, and this time the child did not run away when she spoke to her.

'Where are those flowers you picked yesterday?' She asked, needing something to detain her. 'Did you find out their names?'

'No, *signorina*.' Elena shook her dark head. Then, with a doubtful glance over her shoulder, she added softly: 'Zia Tommasa does not know about the flowers, *signorina*. I hid them in the closet in my bedroom. I am afraid she will be angry when she sees them.'

'She will if she finds them in your closet, Elena.' Suzanne sighed. 'Your father gave you permission to keep them. Zia Tommasa will respect that.'

'Do you think so, *signorina*?' Elena still looked doubtful. 'Papà may have changed his mind.'

'Now why would he do that?'

'I don't know, *signorina*. I only know that today he will not speak to me.'

Suzanne could feel the tautening of her stomach muscles as the child spoke. It was seemingly impossible for her to have the simplest conversation here without bearing the backlash of her own emotions.

'Well. . .' Now she sought for words to reassure the child. 'If—if you like, I'll help you.'

'You, *signorina*?'

'Yes. Yes, me.' Suzanne hoped she was not about to step into even deeper water. 'Do you—that is, does your father have any books that might give us the names of flowers? You know—an encyclopaedia of some sort?'

'Papà has encyclopaedias, *signorina*. I've seen them in his study. Shall I get one?'

'Oh, no—no!' Suzanne halted her urgently, a hand closing round the child's wrist. 'Don't—don't interrupt your father.'

'But he is not in his study, *signorina*.'

'He's not?'

'No, *signorina*. He is working in the Grand Salon.'

'The—Grand Salon?'

'Yes, *signorina*. You have not seen the Grand Salon?'

'No.' Suzanne shook her head.

'Then you must ask Papà to show you,' said Elena firmly. 'He will, if you ask him.' She smiled. 'Papà likes you, *signorina*. I am glad you like him too.'

Suzanne controlled her embarrassment with difficulty. 'About that encyclopaedia, Elena. . .'

But the child was not to be diverted so easily. 'Papà used not to spend so much time alone, *signorina*. He was not always so—so cross. Before his accident, we used to have such fun together.'

Suzanne couldn't help herself. 'And don't you any more?'

Elena shrugged. 'Sometimes,' she admitted with such pathos that all Suzanne's protective instincts were aroused. 'But these days Papà is usually too busy. . .'

'Well. . .' Suzanne sensed that tears were not far away. 'Let's concentrate on the flowers, shall we? You tell me where the encyclopaedia is, and I'll get it while you get the flowers, hmm? We can work for an hour before it's time to change for dinner. Or do you have to have your meal?'

'Not for a while,' Elena answered, obviously tempted by the idea. 'All right, *signorina*. But if Zia Tommasa—'

'I'll handle Zia Tommasa,' said Suzanne, with more bravado than confidence. 'Oh, and Elena, my name's Suzanne. I think we can dispense with *signorina*, don't you?'

Elena nodded eagerly, a smile tilting the corners of her mouth. 'Yes. Yes—Suzanne.'

The intonation in her voice as she said Suzanne's name was reminiscent of the way her father said the word, and Suzanne followed the child into the villa with a rapidly beating heart.

It was nerve-racking raiding Mazzaro's study. But the door was standing wide, and she felt that no one could accuse her of intrusion. The bookshelves were full of reference books of one kind or another, and although they were all written in Italian, it didn't take her long to unearth a rather decrepit edition of *The Compleat Gardener*. There were enough pictures in it to enable them to identify at least some of Elena's plants and they would have to guess the rest.

As she turned to leave, her feet took her towards his desk, her fingers reaching out to touch the polished surface, lingering at the spot where he had rested. Then, as though aware of what construction could be put on her actions if anyone else encountered her there, she quickly left the room.

They spent almost an hour on the loggia, separating the weeds from the genuine flowers, and while they worked they talked, Elena showing an intense interest in Suzanne's way of life, and her work at the hotel. It was obvious the child met few adults outside the occupants of the Villa, and the nuns at the convent where she went to school. She was hungry for information about the world outside the walls of her existence and Suzanne found herself explaining about her parents' broken marriage and her father's subsequent death.

'And you don't mind that your mother married again?' Elena queried, a frown marring the smooth brow, her chin cupped on one small fist.

'Why should I?' Suzanne countered now, flicking over the pages of the gardening manual. 'My parents weren't happy together. Why shouldn't they try for happiness with someone else?'

'But—but Zia Tommasa says there is no divorce. That once people are married, they are married for life.'

'Yes, well. . .' Suzanne looked across at the little girl ruefully. 'Life isn't always that simple. I mean, look at it this way—which do you think is preferable? That two people should spend the life that's left to them in constant conflict with their partners? Or that they should separate and make a new life for themselves?' She sighed. 'It isn't always easy on their children either. It's not very nice listening to arguments day after day, knowing that the future is going to change nothing.'

'But Zia Tommasa says that if people are unhappy, they should ask God to help them.'

Suzanne picked up a tiny pink flower and pointed to a picture in the manual. 'Do you think this is dogwood? It looks a bit like it, doesn't it?'

Elena barely glanced at the illustration. 'Do you think that God wants people to be unhappy?' she persisted.

Suzanne reached across to take her hand. 'Of course not.'

'Because I was thinking, Mamma and Papà are not happy. Perhaps they should get a divorce, hmm?'

Suzanne could feel the hot colour sweeping up her face. 'Oh, now, Elena,' she exclaimed, releasing the child's hand, 'divorce doesn't solve everything.'

'But you said—when two people were unhappy—'

'Elena, I don't know anything about your parents' marriage,' she protested, dreading to think what Mazzaro would say if he could hear this conversation. 'Look, isn't this a spider lily?'

Elena looked dejected. 'I wish—I wish they would get a divorce,' she said through trembling lips. 'I wish Mamma would go away!'

'Elena!'

The child sniffed. 'It's true. I mean it. She doesn't like me, I know that, and she makes Papà so—so moody. They were shouting at each other last night. I—I heard them. Mamma's room is near to mine, and Papà—Papà was there.'

Suzanne determinedly turned another page of the manual. It's getting late, Elena. We're going to have to finish this another day.'

'When? Tomorrow?'

Suzanne bit her lip. 'I suppose it will have to be tomorrow. I'm leaving on Tuesday.'

'You are?' Elena looked dismayed. 'But—but Pietro is here for almost two weeks!'

'Ah, yes, but he's at college, Elena. I have a job of work to do. I'm not allowed to take unlimited free time.'

'But Tuesday!' Elena hunched her shoulders. 'Will you be coming again?'

Suzanne hesitated. But she couldn't completely

disillusion the child. 'I—I don't know,' she answered evasively. 'Maybe.'

The unusual sound of rain against the windows awoke Suzanne on Monday morning. Slipping out of bed, she discovered that the sky was grey and unyielding, a complete contrast to the sunshine of the past three days.

She was dressed in slim pants and an orange shirt when Lucia brought in her breakfast tray, and the old servant looked at her in surprise.

'You wish to take breakfast with the Conte, *signorina*?' she suggested, gesturing towards the door again, but Suzanne shook her head.

'No! That is—no, thank you, Lucia. I—er—I'll have it here now you've brought it.'

'No trouble, *signorina*.'

'No, really. . .' Suzanne softened her words with a faint smile. 'I'm—I'm not feeling very sociable right now.'

Lucia put down the tray and eloquently shrugged her shoulders. 'I have days like that myself, *signorina*. You are sad that it is raining on your last day, *no*?'

Suzanne glanced half absently towards the windows. The weather had little to do with her mood. But it was easier to agree, and Lucia left her muttering her sympathies.

She ate a croissant, drank several cups of strong black coffee, and then wandered back to the windows. Rain pattered on the balcony outside, and the fountain in the courtyard looked bedraggled and forlorn. Was it only the rain which was making her feel so depressed? Or was it the knowledge that in a little over twenty-four hours she would be leaving the Villa, and would probably never see either it or its inhabitants again? And if that was so, why was she skulking up here when the man she most wanted to see was eating his breakfast alone downstairs? Ignoring the dictates of her conscience, she walked quickly to the door and left the room.

Her courage almost failed her at the door to the dining room. After the way she had spoken to him two nights ago, he might well wish to avoid her, and just because she was prepared to overlook her shortcomings, he might not.

She tapped at the panels and waited with bated breath. There was no immediate response, and she was tempted to turn away. But Lucia had said he was having breakfast and this was where he ate. Taking a deep breath, she pressed down on the iron handle of one of the doors and it opened a fraction, permitting her a glimpse of Mazzaro alone at the table, reading his newspaper.

Another breath, and the door was wide enough to allow her to slide into the room, and she closed it again by leaning back against it. The click it made attracted Mazzaro's attention at last, and he looked up half impatiently, his expression becoming guarded when he saw who it was. He laid his paper politely aside, however, and holding on to the table, drew himself to his feet.

'Good morning,' he greeted her, without warmth. 'Are you joining me?'

'I—no,' Suzanne moved awkwardly away from

the door. 'I—I have eaten.' She gestured involuntarily. 'Please, *signore*, sit down. I—I didn't come to—to interrupt you.'

Mazzaro's brows descended. 'Then why are you here, Miss Hunt?'

Suzanne sighed. 'Oh, all right, I—I suppose I am interrupting you, aren't I? But—well, I wanted to apologise.'

'To apologise, Miss Hunt?'

He wasn't making it easy for her, and she wished he would sit down so that at least that feeling of inadequacy would be removed. '*Signore*, the other evening. . .'

'Saturday evening?'

'Yes. Yes. Saturday evening. I—well, you offered to show me round the Villa on Sunday morning, and I—I rather rudely refused. . .'

'You were going to Mass, as I recall.'

'Yes. Yes, I was. But—well, I leave tomorrow, *signore*, and I wondered if there was any chance. . .'

'. . .that you might see the collection today?'

'Yes.'

Mazzaro's mouth twisted. 'I regret, *signorina*, I have an appointment in Muvano this morning.'

'Oh!' Suzanne nodded. She should have known. What conceit to imagine that the Conte di Falcone could adjust his schedules to accommodate her. 'Well, I—I just wanted to say I—I'm sorry for turning you down. . .'

'Not an uncommon occurrence for me, *signorina*. Think nothing of it.' Mazzaro at last subsided into his seat again. 'Was that all?'

Suzanne pressed her lips together to prevent them from trembling, and nodded her head, not trusting herself to speak.

Mazzaro crumbled a roll on his plate. 'I understand I have to thank you for taking an interest in Elena while you've been here,' he commented. 'She tells me that you and she spent some time together yesterday cataloguing the flowers she gathered.'

'I—I enjoyed it.' Suzanne shifted her weight from one foot to the other. 'I—I hope you didn't object to us borrowing the gardening manual from your study.'

Mazzaro looked steadily across at her. 'What if I were to tell you that you can take anything you want from me?' he asked quietly.

Suzanne gasped. 'I—' She swallowed convulsively. 'I—don't know what you mean, *signore*.'

'No?' He pushed back his chair and rose to his feet again. 'That was not my impression a few moments ago when you entered this room.'

Suzanne moved her shoulders helplessly. 'I—I wanted to apologise. . .'

He left his sticks where they were and came round the table towards her. In tight-fitting hide pants and a loosely-fitting tunic of purple silk embroidered with a black motif, he was an imposing adversary, every bit as intimidating as his Medici ancestors must have been. His scarred face only added to the illusion, and Suzanne felt like retreating before such controlled self-possession.

Mazzaro halted before her, looking down at her intently. 'I do not know what you expect from me, Suzanne, but I think you are not unaware of a certain—affinity between us, *no*?'

'Your—your sticks,' she stammered, and he uttered an oath.

'*Dio*, Suzanne, must you always concern yourself with my incapacities? Is that how you see me? As a broken creature, past its prime, strung together with catgut, deluding itself that it is still a man?'

'No,' she cried vehemently. 'Oh, Mazzaro. . .'

Her hand reached out of its own accord and touched his fingers, a shiver of excitement sliding down her spine as his hand closed over hers, bringing her palm to his lips.

His eyes sought hers as his tongue probed the tiny pores exposed to his caress, and then he drew her hand towards him, unbuttoning his tunic and pushing her fingers inside against his hard-muscled body. Suzanne's lips parted as her breathing accelerated, and when his eyes dropped to the trembling softness of her mouth, it was almost a physical assault on her senses.

'Suzanne.' He said her name hoarsely, his accent thickening with emotion, and the realisation that she was arousing him as much as he was arousing her was an intoxicating conception. Her eyes lowered to encompass the whole length of him. At any moment, he was going to draw her into his arms, she thought unsteadily. He would press her close against the lean intimacy of his thighs, she could almost feel his muscles straining against hers, and if he kissed her—

With a choking effort that took every ounce of will power she dragged herself away from him, putting some space between them before saying stumblingly: 'I—I must go. I—I have packing to do. . .'

Mazzaro flexed his shoulder muscles almost wearily, and there were lines of strain around the thinning line of his mouth which had not been there before. Then, flatly, he said: 'I will postpone my appointment in Muvano, Suzanne.'

His words brought her head up with a jerk. 'Post—postpone your appointment?'

'That's right.' His voice was clipped, and he limped rather heavily back to the table to collect his sticks. 'Forgive me,' he added, indicating the steel canes. 'I spent too long on my legs yesterday, and I'm afraid today I am paying for it.'

'Mazzaro. . .'

His eyes were cool as he surveyed her questioningly. Then he said: 'Do not alarm yourself, Suzanne. It is not my intention to take advantage of your interest in my collection. However, as you are leaving tomorrow, I am prepared to forgo my visit to the museum in Muvano.' He paused. 'Unless of course you have lost interest in seeing the rest of the Villa.'

Suzanne shifted uncomfortably. Lost interest? She hadn't lost interest. But was that really what was at issue? She believed Mazzaro when he said he had no intention of taking advantage of her. But could she trust herself? The knowledge that after today she might never see him again was tearing her to pieces.

'Of course, if you have changed your mind. . .'

Changed her mind? 'Oh, no. No!' Suzanne stared at him fretfully. 'Mazzaro, do you think you should. . .'

He turned his back on her. 'I have to make a telephone call—to Paolo Terrini, explaining that I shall not be coming to Muvano this morning.' He glanced at her briefly over his shoulder. 'I will meet you in the hall in fifteen minutes.'

Suzanne hesitated only a moment before letting herself out of the door. But in her room, she wished she did not continually persist in making life difficult for herself. Yet, as she looked at her flushed cheeks and the softly curving vulnerability of her mouth, she knew she was deluding herself by imagining she had any real control over what was happening to her.

The long gallery on the opposite side of the building echoed hollowly to the sound of Mazzaro's sticks. Tall columns, like those on the other side of the Villa, were inset with a selection of the paintings about which Pietro had spoken so bitterly. That some were a record of Mazzaro's ancestry meant less than their exquisite execution, their skilled interpretation defying valuation. Names like Giorgione and Veronese, Masaccio and Bellini fell carelessly from Mazzaro's tongue, but Suzanne hardly absorbed a third of what he told her, in spite of the mask of detachment he had resumed.

In an alcove, a canvas depicting a group of figures was individually lighted, and she read the words *Michelangelo da Caravaggio*.

'Caravaggio was the man who virtually revolutionised Italian painting in the sixteenth century,' Mazzaro explained, with the practised jargon of a guide. 'His conception of light and colour infused his work with an almost tangible reality. *Chiaroscuro*.'

'Light and dark,' translated Suzanne in surprise, and Mazzaro nodded.

'That was not Caravaggio's only claim to fame— or perhaps notoriety is a better description,' he went on. 'He aroused a great deal of dissension by his insistence on interpreting religious scenes in a contemporary style, depicting Biblical characters with dirty feet and sweaty faces. As you can imagine, his work did not find favour with the Church.'

'I wonder why he did it.'

Mazzaro shrugged. 'Because that was how he saw it, one presumes, After all, it would be foolish to suppose that Joseph's feet did not get dirty on the road to Nazareth, or that Christ Himself did not sweat in the heat of the day, dragging that heavy cross through the streets of Jerusalem.'

'Perhaps Caravaggio thought people might more easily identify with things they knew and understood.'

'Undoubtedly he did. In that respect he was way ahead of his time. But Christ thought that, too, and look what they did to Him.'

'But you can't compare—' Suzanne broke off abruptly, looking up at him. 'I thought you didn't go to church.'

'I don't. But that is not to say I don't find merit in Christian beliefs.' His eyes narrowed. 'Shall we go on?'

Suzanne was prepared for the size of the rooms they entered, but not for their ornate decoration.

Modelled stucco, gilded ceilings, cupids reclining among fruit and garlands, mirrors losing their identity in scrolls and arabesques; wall paintings between pillars of veined marble that still possessed the clarity of their original expression. Rooms opened one from the other, curved archways or square doors set in line with one another, so that each appeared to be a reflection of the last. There were ceiling paintings and frescoed panels, and entwining chandeliers, and seemingly acres of variegated marble underfoot.

Some of the rooms were empty but for glass cases, and the largest of these, the Grand Salon, contained Mazzaro's collection of gold and silver. There were coins and precious stones, and medals set in bronze and silver and gold symbolising various important personages. Mazzaro explained that later these medals were minted as mementoes of a child's birth or a wedding, and used as calling cards.

But it was the rooms which were furnished that intrigued Suzanne most. The flamboyantly painted chairs and tables, cabinets of ebony and walnut, with carved decorations or inlaid with marble and *pietra dura*, enchanted her, particularly as the velvet cords which kept the public at bay had been removed, and she was able to touch and handle things at close quarters.

'I think the purpose of furniture made between the fourteenth and seventeenth centuries meant less than its form,' commented Mazzaro dryly, as Suzanne admired the moulded panelling of a carved *cassone*, or marriage chest. 'Designers used to pay little attention to their patrons' comfort, you know. These chairs, for example—I shouldn't care to try and squeeze myself between these fragile arms, and do you honestly think these legs would support my weight?'

Suzanne had to smile. 'But you're not a typical Italian, are you, Mazzaro?' she exclaimed impulsively, and then felt her knees grow weak at the look in his eyes.

'Am I not?'

She turned away to hide her emotion, saying rather nervously: 'Men—Italian men—are usually smaller, are—aren't they?'

'Smallness is not necessarily a physical condition,' he commented dryly. 'Shall we go upstairs?'

'Upstairs?' Suzanne turned to face him then. 'Are the—bedrooms opened to the public?'

'No. But if you would care to see them. . .I warn you, they'll be covered in dust, in spite of Lucia's ministrations.'

Suzanne's spine tingled. 'I—I don't mind.'

'Very well.'

Expecting they would have to return to the central hall to mount the staircase to the first floor, Suzanne was intrigued when Mazzaro led her through doors at the end of the gallery which revealed a second, steeper flight of stairs.

Transferring both his sticks to one hand, he indicated that she should precede him, saying wryly: 'At least this way I don't have to concern myself with unseen eyes, *no*?'

The upper gallery resembled the gallery which gave Suzanne access to her bedroom, although the

drawn blinds added an eerie shadowness to the
vaulted ceiling. Mazzaro released one of the blinds
so that she could look out over the tiled roofs of the
village below them to the valley beyond. He stood
beside her in the window embrasure, and the heated
scent of his body drifted to her nostrils, making her
intensely aware of him. Aware, too, that if she moved
her head, her hair would brush his shoulder. But he
moved away, and she breathed more freely as she
followed him along the corridor to the first of the
bedrooms.

White dust-sheets shrouded gilded chairs and
tables, and long-obsolete commodes, with exotically
painted birds on their panels. Mazzaro half smiled
at Suzanne's evident embarrassment when she discovered their use, and flung aside the sheet which
concealed the faded embroidery of the coverlet on
the bed. Fraying curtains, which must once have surrounded the bed and protected its occupants from
draughts, were suspended from the carved ceiling,
and Mazzaro told her that until the fifteenth century
beds had had neither headboards nor posts.

He had not been joking when he had said that the
rooms would be dusty. Cobwebs hung in every
corner, and she dreaded to think what enormous spid-
ers must lurk within their webs. It seemed a tragedy
that so much that was beautiful went unseen here
purely through lack of finance, and a desire on
Mazzaro's part to remain independent.

Room followed room and in every one there was
some object of interest: gilded stools with worn seats,
chipped chests and shredded tapestries, enamelled

vases that were cracked or their glazing scratched. Some of the rooms had a musty smell as if it was years since anyone had opened them up, and Suzanne began to feel an increasing nostalgia for the days when the Falcone family had the fortune and the staff to maintain the villa. Here, more than anywhere else, she was conscious of the gulf which stretched between her life and the life of the Falcones.

Mazzaro seemed to sense her feelings. 'What are you thinking?' he asked quietly.

To tell him would have been too revealing a reflection of the direction her thoughts were taking. Instead, she fingered the tasselled fringing of a bedspread, and shaking her head, said carelessly: 'I—I was just wondering what people used to wear to go to bed. I mean—' She coloured. 'Before nightshirts and things.'

'Until the sixteenth century, I believe people generally slept naked,' Mazzaro replied, with disconcerting candour, supporting himself against the bedpost, his sticks superfluous for the moment. 'Unless they were cold, I suppose, and then they didn't bother to undress.'

'I see.' Suzanne moistened her upper lip.

'Does that shock you?'

She gave him an indignant look. 'No. Why should it?'

He shrugged. 'I thought you looked as if it had.'

'Well, I didn't.' She shifted, making an offhand gesture. 'Good heavens, that's nothing new.'

'Agreed.' He inclined his head. 'My apologies.'

Suzanne pressed her lips together frustratedly. 'I

didn't mean it like that.' she exclaimed. 'Oh—' She turned away to assume an interest in a tulipwood *escritoire*. 'This is pretty. Is it French?'

She felt him move across the floor to join her, his shoulder brushing hers as he bent to open the tiny drawers, revealing a hidden compartment behind one of them.

'Yes, it's French,' he said, straightening as she did the same, and their breath intermingled. His tortured enunciation of her name was an extension of her own longing, a need that had been growing every moment they were together. Almost in slow motion, she felt his hands descending on her shoulders, and the exquisite cruelty of his grasp was no more than a needlepoint in the agony of emotion she was experiencing. He bent his head, and her eyes closed against the burning darkness of his, his lips stroking hers apart before capturing her mouth.

It was like sailing out into the middle of a lake and suddenly finding your craft had given way, Suzanne thought afterwards. All the kisses and casual embraces she had endured had been as nothing compared to Mazzaro's love-making. He stirred the deepest depths of her being arousing emotions that frightened her by their intensity. His hands slid over her shoulder blades to her hips, drawing her intimately against him, and the pressure of his mouth increased when he felt her instinctive withdrawal.

'Suzanne,' he groaned, 'what did you expect? I'm only a man!'

She moved her head helplessly from side to side. 'I know, I know—'

'Don't be afraid of me, Suzanne.'

'I'm—not afraid of you—'

'Aren't you?' Her eyes opened to the bitterness in his voice. 'Perhaps you ought to be.'

'Oh, Mazzaro!' she breathed, his nearness weakening what small reserve was left to her. 'Mazzaro, don't make me care about you—'

His mouth silenced her protest, and this time she yielded against him, luxuriating in the hard strength of his body straining against hers. But they were not close enough. She was supremely conscious of the bed just beside them, and of how desirable it would be to lie there in Mazzaro's arms, feeling the masculine roughness of his skin against hers. . .

At last, Mazzaro lifted his head to rest his forehead on hers. She felt no sense of embarrassment now in the continuing closeness of his body, but his eyes were heavy-lidded as he looked down at her.

'We have to get out of here,' he told her huskily.

'I know. . .'

'I'm not going to apologise.'

'I don't want you to.'

'You know I want to make love to you.'

'Yes.'

'So I have to let you go.'

'Do you?'

His eyes darkened. 'Suzanne, you told me—'

'I know. It's true. But—I've never—never—'

She couldn't finish, her fingers going involuntarily to the buttons of his tunic, unfastening them tremblingly, revealing the pelt of dark hair which ran down to his navel. Mazzaro looked down at what she was doing, and then with a groan he caught her hands in one of his, swiftly refastening the buttons and putting her away from him.

'Mazzaro. . .' she whispered painfully, and he raked an angry hand through his hair.

'I'm only human, Suzanne,' he muttered thickly. 'How far do you think I can go?'

Suzanne drew a deep breath. 'You're not— angry?'

'Angry?' He gave her an old-fashioned look. 'Dear God, Suzanne, I am trying to be sane!' He limped to where he had left his sticks, and grasped them determinedly in both hands. 'Shall we go?'

Suzanne sighed. 'Is it necessary to use those sticks now?' she exclaimed, half impatiently. 'You don't really need them, do you? I mean, just now. . . What are they? A defence? A barrier? Something to keep other people at bay?'

Mazzaro regarded her unsmilingly. 'Don't try to psycho-analyse me, Suzanne.'

'I'm not. But I think there's some truth in what I've said. Why do you do it, Mazzaro? Is it—is it because of your face?'

'Suzanne!'

His tone was grim, but she stared at him frustratedly. 'Mazzaro, if they're not necessary. . . Why keep up the pretence?' She spread her hands wide. 'You have so much else!'

'I know. A crumbling villa propping up a crumbling marriage.'

'That needn't be so. You could—get a divorce.'

'Not a chance!' he stated coldly. 'Not in this

family. Don't get the wrong impression from me, Suzanne, marriage—will not enter into our relationship.'

His words stung. 'I haven't suggested that it should!'

'No.' He inclined his head. 'No, you have not. And no doubt I am being presumptuous as usual in mentioning it, but however much I might desire you, Suzanne, I could never—what do you say in your country?—make an honest woman of you, *no*?'

She ought to have expected nothing less than complete candour from him. That was the kind of man he was; one of the things she found most attractive about him. But his words were cold comfort to the rapidly cooling ardour of her emotions. It hardly seemed possible that moments ago he had been trembling in her arms, when now he seemed so— so aloof!

And yet he must always have been in control. That day by the falls, and now here. It was galling. If only she could say the same! Why was it, when on every other occasion in her life when she had been faced with an emotional situation she had remained totally unmoved by appeals, with this man she had no defence? His words hurt her, but his indifference was worse. A stirring sense of resentment came to her assistance, and with it an anger that made her say indignantly:

'You mentioned your crumbling marriage, not me!'

His eyebrows ascended. 'We will not discuss it, I think.'

'Won't we?' Suzanne straightened her spine. 'Why not?'

'Suzanne, let us not get involved in futile argument. I am sorry if I have done anything to offend you—'

'Offend me?' She stared at him disbelievingly. 'Oh, come on! You've just made love to me in a way that no man has ever been allowed to do before, and you're sorry if you've offended me!'

'I did not make love to you. I kissed you.'

'Is that what you call it? I got the impression there was more to it than that—'

'Suzanne, stop it!'

'Stop what? Isn't it *de rigueur* to discuss the sordid details?'

'They were not sordid, Suzanne!'

'No?' She was alarmed at the pleasure she was gaining out of hurting him. 'But you'd prefer not to be reminded.'

The lines of his face were deeply carved etchings of the anger he was controlling. 'Suzanne, I have tried to explain—'

'And what am I supposed to say? Pull my forelock, and say: *That's all right, your lordship, sir, think nothing of it*?'

Mazzaro took a threatening step towards her, and then drew back abruptly. 'I think it is time we went downstairs,' he stated coldly. 'It's obvious that indulging in a slanging match is going to do no good whatsoever.'

Suzanne's chin trembled, but she controlled it with difficulty. 'Of course,' she said tremulously, 'I'd forgotten your countrymen's reputation! It wouldn't do for you to let the side down, would it?'

'Suzanne. . .'

There was weary resignation in his voice now, and her fleeting sense of triumph fled in the face of his defeat.

'Oh, Mazzaro,' she exclaimed huskily, 'why did you do it?'

He looked at her for a long disturbing minute, and then he turned away. 'Come. It is after twelve. Pietro will be wondering where you are.'

'I don't care about Pietro. . .'

'Then perhaps you should.' He looked at her over his shoulder as he limped towards the door. 'Didn't he tell you? Unless by some miracle I produce a son, one day all this will be his!'

CHAPTER EIGHT

'WE have a party of thirty Americans coming in next Tuesday, Suzanne. They already have a schedule planned—you know, the usual thing, places of historical interest, museums, art galleries and so on. But I'd like you to arrange a couple of theatre visits for them. Can you do that?'

'Yes, Mr Norton,' Suzanne looked up at the hotel manager from her seat behind the desk in her small office. 'Have they any particular preference?'

'Well. . .' He considered for a moment. 'I suppose it depends what's available really. But if you can fix up a musical of some sort and perhaps some straight theatre, that would be ideal. The play at the Shaftesbury has had some good reviews, but I expect it's fully booked for the next three months.'

'All right, I'll see what I can do.'

'Good.' Malcolm Norton was about to turn away when another thought struck him. 'Suzanne, I don't want you to think I'm an interfering old fool, but— are you all right?'

'Me?' She gave a careless shrug of her shoulders, playing for time. 'Of course I'm all right. Why do you ask?'

'I don't know.' The grey-haired man in front of her frowned. 'But since you came back from Italy last month, I've frequently thought how pale you've been looking. Did you pick up a bug out there or something?'

'Heavens, no.' Suzanne bent her head, shuffling the papers on her desk. 'There's nothing wrong with me.' She forced her head up, knowing he would suspect averted eyes. 'I—well, it's been a particularly hot spell, you know, and I suppose I'm just feeling the strain.'

Malcolm Norton remained sceptical. 'And it's nothing to do with the fact that you've stopped seeing that young man of yours?' he probed.

'No.' Suzanne sighed, although this at least was safer ground. 'Mr Norton, Pietro and I were just friends, that's all. And—well, you know what it's like. Spending a lot of time with someone—it can change things.'

'Familiarity breeding contempt?'

'Something like that.'

He paused. 'It hasn't to do with Fezik, has it?'

Suzanne shook her head. 'He's been away.'

'I know, I know. But he's been back a few days now, and I thought he might be starting to—well, you didn't like his attentions, did you?'

'You knew?'

'Of course I knew. But there was nothing I could do. I mean, the man's a personal friend of old Stassis, you know. I believe his mother or his grandmother was some relation to the old boy's cousin, and family ties are pretty strong out there.'

'I know that.'

'Besides, he's not such an ogre, you know.' The manager moved towards the door. 'But you do what you want, and don't work so hard, do you hear? I don't want to lose my assistant through ill health. You take it easy.'

'Yes, Mr Norton.'

But after her superior had left her, Suzanne got up from her desk and moved to the windows of her office, which overlooked the busy thoroughfare adjoining Oxford Street. That was the trouble, she thought wearily. Since she had returned to London, life had been too easy; she had had too much time to brood about what had happened at Castelfalcone. Maybe if it had been the Christmas season, or the hotel had been filled to overflowing, she would have had plenty to occupy her mind. But London was quiet for the height of the season, and she had too much time on her hands.

She had not laid eyes on Pietro since her return. He had telephoned once, perfunctorily she had thought, and as they had not parted on the best of terms she had had no real compunction about breaking with him. He had seemed ridiculously immature after Mazzaro, although in effect he was as old as she was, and the rebuff she had delivered him before leaving Italy had aroused his pride as well as his temper.

In consequence, her evenings were her own. She had lost touch with most of her girl-friends through spending so much time abroad, and as she preferred not to go out alone, her small apartment had become her prison. She felt almost despairing at times, knowing that this was a situation she had never experienced before. Misery at the thought of never

seeing Mazzaro again stalked her at all times, made
all the more poignant by disgust at the remembrance
of her behaviour. What memories must Mazzaro hold
of her, arguing with him so spitefully, reducing their
relationship to a slanging match? She shivered, and
turned back to her desk. It was no use torturing herself with thoughts like that, even though she knew
that unless she found justification for her actions,
she would never be free again.

Her mother telephoned her the following evening.

'Suzanne? Suzanne dear, is that you?'

'Who did you expect to find at this number,
Mummy?' inquired her daughter with wry humour.
'Yes, it's me. How are you?'

'I'm coming up to town on Thursday, Suzanne. Is
there any chance of us having lunch together?'

Suzanne welcomed the prospect. 'Of course,' she
exclaimed. 'Where shall we meet?'

'How about the Grillroom? They always serve
such a delicious prawn cocktail. And we can
talk there.'

'All right,' Suzanne agreed. 'What time?'

They decided that one o'clock would be most suitable, but it was almost twenty past before Annabel
Forrest came hurrying across to Suzanne's table.

'Oh, dear! I'm sorry to keep you waiting,
Suzanne,' her mother exclaimed apologetically, 'but
I've been having my hair styled, and you know how
long they can take!'

'It looks very nice,' responded Suzanne dutifully,
as her mother seated herself. 'Now, do you want a
drink first, or shall I order the meal?'

'Oh, order the meal, darling. I'm ravenous. I haven't eaten a thing since yesterday evening, and the coffee I had on the train was positively putrid!'

Suzanne summoned the waiter, and knowing her mother's preference, gave their order.

'Let's have a bottle of Riesling with our meal,' suggested Mrs Forrest, as the waiter was departing, and he promised to send the wine waiter to them.

'What is all this about?' asked Suzanne, in surprise. 'A new hair style, and now a whole bottle of wine for lunch! What are we celebrating?'

'Neil's just won the contract to design the new comprehensive school!' her mother announced proudly. 'And as a special treat, next week we're going to Germany. A Rhine cruise, can you imagine it? I've not been so excited since our honeymoon.'

Her mother's second husband was an architect in Bristol. But he was a dour Scotsman, and his penchant for saving money had been the cause of many a row between them. However, it seemed his good fortune was mellowing his meanness.

'I'm so pleased for you.' Suzanne squeezed her mother's hand gently. 'You deserve a holiday. You haven't had one for years.'

'I know. But Neil is always so busy. . .'

Suzanne could have added that he was never too busy to play golf or go out for a day's fishing, but she didn't. It was sufficient to know that for once her mother had no grievances.

During the meal, they talked about general topics, but eventually, noticing how little Suzanne was actually eating, Mrs Forrest brought out the same observation Malcolm Norton had used a few days before.

'You're looking awfully pale, Suzanne. Are you feeling well?'

Suzanne made an impatient gesture. I'm perfectly well, thank you.'

'But you're hardly eating a thing.'

'It's too hot to eat.'

Her mother glanced round the restaurant. 'It is hot in here, I agree. I don't know why these places can't all be air-conditioned. I mean, they charge enough, in all conscience.' Then she transferred her attention back to her daughter. 'But the heat's never bothered you before, has it? You couldn't work in places like—like Athens, and Rimini, without being able to stand hot weather.'

Suzanne raised her wine glass to her lips. 'Does it matter?'

'Of course it matters.' Mrs Forrest regarded her anxiously. 'You're not—you haven't—I mean, you haven't done anything silly, have you, darling?'

Suzanne's lips hardened. 'Like—get myself pregnant, do you mean?

Mrs Forrest glanced about her apprehensively. 'Keep your voice down, Suzanne. We don't want half the restaurant listening to our conversation.'

Suzanne sighed, and replaced her glass on the table. 'Mummy, I'm not that stupid!' But wasn't she? 'Besides, these days it's not necessary to run those kind of risks. There is the pill, you know.'

'The pill!' Mrs Forrest dabbed at her mouth with her napkin. 'And what do they really know about

the pill, I ask you? No one's taken it long enough
to know what the eventual effects might be.'

'Maybe not. But I'd rather take the pill if I had to
than run the risk of an unwanted pregnancy.'

'Suzanne!' Her mother stared at her in dismay.
'Are you telling me you—you sleep with these men
you go out with?'

Suzanne gave an exasperated exclamation. 'No.
No, Mummy, that's not what I'm saying at all.'

Mrs Forrest sniffed. 'I think it's dreadful the way
young girls go in for that sort of thing. I mean, by
the time they get married, there's nothing they don't
know.' She flicked a glance at her daughter. 'I never
thought you were like that, Suzanne.'

'I'm not!' Suzanne felt impatient. 'Oh, for
heaven's sake, let's change the subject.'

'Well, if you're not pregnant, what is wrong with
you?' demanded her mother fretfully. 'I may not
have been the most devoted of mothers, Suzanne,
but I know when you're not yourself.'

'Do you?' Suzanne looked across at the dessert
trolley, loaded down with fresh raspberries and
strawberries, meringues and brandy snaps, and dishes
of sherry trifle, and felt rather sick. 'Well, I can only
repeat, I'm fine.'

'What happened at Easter?'

'At Easter?' Suzanne's head jerked back to her
mother's. 'What do you mean—what happened at
Easter?'

'Don't bite my head off, darling.' Mrs Forrest
looked hurt. 'I'm not the Gestapo, you know. Only
you usually come down and see us over the holiday

weekend, and when you didn't this year, I rang and couldn't get in touch with you. The receptionist didn't know where you were. She just told me you weren't in the hotel.'

'Oh, I see.' Suzanne assumed a sudden interest in her wine glass, stroking her finger round the rim. 'No—well, I was away, actually.'

'Away? Away where? With whom?'

Suzanne considered making up some story, but it simply wasn't worth the effort.

'As a matter of fact I was in Italy,' she conceded reluctantly. 'Staying with the family of a young Italian student I used to go out with.'

'In Italy? With some student's family?' Mrs Forrest looked horrified. 'And you didn't think to tell us where you were going!'

'It was a spur of the moment thing,' said Suzanne defensively. 'At first I said I couldn't go, but then— well, it was a change.'

'A change!' Her mother shook her head disgust-edly. 'I suppose because you've lived in Italy, you think you know all there is to know about Italians.'

'No.' Suzanne looked up. 'But Pietro is—well, he's from a good family. There was no—harm in it.'

'Pietro!' Her mother scoffed. 'Pietro what?'

'Vitale.'

'Where does he come from?'

'Does it matter, Mummy?' Suzanne swallowed a gulp of wine. 'Our—relationship is over. I shan't be seeing him again.'

'Is that why you're looking so down-in-the-mouth?'

'How many more times? I am not down-in-the-mouth.'

'Well, I don't believe you, Suzanne.' Her mother nodded annoyingly, as if in comprehension. 'I knew there was something wrong. Well, I shouldn't worry over any unreliable—'

'Mother, *please*!'

The tone of Suzanne's voice got through to her, and Mrs Forrest looked offended. 'What's the matter?' she protested. 'What did I say? I'm only trying to comfort you.'

'I don't need comforting.' Suzanne's lips were tight. 'Now, what are you going to have as a dessert?'

Mrs Forrest decided on the cheesecake, and just to placate her, Suzanne accepted a small helping of the sherry trifle. But its sweetness was cloying, and she had the utmost difficulty in swallowing any of it.

Then, just when she thought the moment of crisis was over, her mother produced her handkerchief, and dabbed pathetically at her eyes.

'What's happened to us, Suzie?' she asked, in the voice Suzanne had grown to despair the sound of in the days when her parents were living together. 'Why don't we talk to one another any more?'

'We do talk to one another!' exclaimed Suzanne desperately, unable to remain immune from her mother's distress. 'We're talking now. . .'

'Yes. But you know you're not telling me everything,' Mrs Forrest gulped tremulously. 'Don't you know that I worry about you, living here in London, on your own—'

'I live in the hotel, Mummy.'

'In your own apartment. That's not the same thing, is it? And then living abroad all that time. . .'

'Oh, Mummy, stop it!' Suzanne pushed her trifle aside. 'I'm perfectly capable of taking care of myself.'

But was she? If Mazzaro had chosen to take advantage of her, if he had lain with her on that bed as she had imagined him doing, what could she have done? And as at no time had she found the need to take those kind of precautions, she might easily have become pregnant. . .

Her mother dried her eyes. 'Well, all I can say is, I'm glad you're not still involved with a foreigner. Good heavens, what kind of a life would you have had, married to an Italian?'

'It was nothing like that, Mummy.'

But her mother ignored her. 'They don't practise birth control, you know,' she went on. 'Oh, no, no pills for them. They just take what comes and thank God for it.'

'Oh, Mummy!' Suzanne had to smile at her mother's homespun philosophy. 'How do you know what Italians do? You shouldn't believe everything you read in magazines.'

'Huh!' Her mother put the last mouthful of cheesecake into her mouth, relishing every morsel. Clearly, her tears had not spoiled her appetite. 'You mark my words, Suzanne. You're better out of it.'

But had she ever been in it? Suzanne asked herself bitterly. Pietro was a boy. She could never imagine herself marrying anyone like him, whatever their nationality. And Mazzaro. . .

She summoned the waiter to order coffee. Her mother would be even more horrified if she told her that she had become infatuated with a married man, particularly if she added that he was an Italian, too. . .

Back at the hotel, Suzanne determinedly put such disruptive thoughts aside. She was dialling the number of a travel agency to make an inquiry for one of their guests when her office door opened to admit the burly figure of a man in his early forties, his swarthy features softening with indulgence.

'Mr Fezik!' Her exclamation hid her apprehension at his unexpected intrusion into her life again. 'I— is there something I can do for you?'

Abdul Fezik gave himself a few minutes to study her before replying, obviously finding her extreme fairness much to his liking. Then he came to rest the palms of his hands on her desk.

'There is much you could do for me, Miss Hunt,' he told her, fiercely. 'But you seem more than a little reluctant to help me.'

Suzanne rose to her feet, replacing the telephone receiver without finishing dialling the number. 'Mr Fezik, I am rather busy. If there's something in particular you want ..'

Fezik straightened, one hand going to adjust his too-tight collar. 'You are outspoken, Miss Hunt. Very well, I shall be, too. I have tickets for the Abinieri concert at the Festival Hall.' He flung an envelope on to her desk. 'I want you to come with me.'

Suzanne expelled her breath on a sigh, ignoring the envelope. Not again! 'Mr Fezik, I—when is this concert?'

'This evening?'

She made an apologetic gesture. 'I'm sorry. My mother's in town today.' That, at least, was true. 'And I'm seeing her this evening. . .' crossing her fingers behind her back.

'Indeed?' Fezik's lips thinned. 'What a pity it was not tomorrow evening, no?'

Suzanne hesitated. Was it a trap? 'Well. . .' she temporised, and be pounced.

'As it happens, the tickets are for tomorrow evening, Miss Hunt,' he stated with a triumphant air. 'I was only—teasing you.'

Suzanne prayed for the telephone to ring, anything to cause a diversion and give her time to marshal her objections.

'Mr Fezik, it's very kind of you to ask me, but—'

'You are not going to turn me down again!' He stared at her angrily. 'What is wrong with me, Miss Hunt? Why do you persistently refuse my invitations? Are you a racialist? I would not have thought so, judging by the skin of the young man you were courting so ardently before your holiday in Italy, no?'

'It's nothing like that, Mr Fezik.'

'Then what?'

'I am not encouraged to conduct relationships with guests at the hotel,' she answered evasively.

'Why not?'

'Oh, Mr Fezik, I have work to do—'

A knock at her door gave her sudden release, and she went to open it eagerly, staring in amazement at the man who was waiting outside. 'Carlo!' she exclaimed. 'I mean—Signor Bottega!'

'Carlo will do,' he remarked, a lazy smile lifting the corners of his mouth. 'So Elena was right. She has a remarkable memory, that child.'

'Elena?' Now that her initial relief at the interruption of her *tête-à-tête* with Abdul Fezik was wearing off, other anxieties took its place. What was Carlo doing here? And what had Elena to do with it?

The man behind her cleared his throat as if to remind her of his presence, and she swung round awkwardly. 'Oh—yes, Mr Fezik. Is—is there anything else?'

Fezik glowered at her. 'You tell me, Miss Hunt.'

Suzanne bit her lip. 'About tomorrow evening. . .I'm afraid it's out of the question. . .'

With a muttered imprecation, Fezik brushed past her, almost knocking Carlo Bottega aside as he stormed out of the door. Carlo stared after him indignantly, and then turned to Suzanne again. 'What is going on?'

'Oh—nothing.' Suzanne stood aside. 'Won't you come in?'

Carlo entered her small office, looking about him approvingly. 'Hmm, very nice.'

Suzanne closed the door, and then she said urgently: 'Elena. You mentioned Elena. Is something wrong?'

Carlo's eyebrows lifted. 'No. Why? Should there be?'

Suzanne sighed. 'You said—Elena told you— where I was?'

'That's right, she did. You had been talking about your work to her, I believe.'

'Yes, I had.' Suzanne hesitated by her desk. 'But—'

'You are not surprised to see me, are you?' Carlo looked put out. 'Didn't I tell you, I come to London quite often for my company.'

'Well, yes, but—'

'I thought you would know.' Carlo's eyes darkened. 'A beautiful girl like you—you must have many invitations.'

Suzanne licked her lips. 'Your—er—I mean, it was hardly an invitation. . .'

But it had been, she realised that now. And Mazzaro had been right.

'It would have been tactless for me to put it into so many words at the time,' said Carlo wryly. 'Wouldn't it?'

She knew what he meant. With Sophia looking on—listening. . .

'Are—are you in London for long, Signor Bottega?' she asked quickly, no more eager to get involved in a relationship with him than she had been with Abdul Fezik.

'I am here for a week, no more, I regret to say.' Carlo shook his head. 'But that is seven days and nights. Two people can get to know one another very well in that time.'

Suzanne backed away behind her desk. 'Oh, please. . .' She smoothed her palms together. 'I'm afraid I don't have a lot of free time.'

Carlo frowned. 'Come, you do not work evenings.'

'Sometimes I do. And—and in any case, I have other—other engagements.'

Carlo looked angry now. 'But I have made a special journey here to see you, Suzanne. You were not so offhand in Italy.'

Suzanne sank down into her seat. 'I'm not being offhand, *signore*. But, I understood you to be rather—friendly with the Contessa.'

It was not polite to mention such things, but at least now Carlo looked slightly disconcerted. 'Sophia and I are friends, yes,' he agreed quickly.

Suzanne gathered confidence. '*Close* friends, *signore*.'

Carlo stiffened, and then as if realising the futility of denying it, he gave a rueful smile. 'All right, all right, *cara*. Sophia and I are—very close friends. But Sophia is in Italy, and you are here!'

The gall of the man! Suzanne stared at him in amazement. Did he think she would be flattered by that statement? First Abdul Fezik, and now Carlo. Why did men always assume that if a woman had passable looks, all she wanted was a good time?

'I can't go out with you, Signor Bottega,' she said at last, definitely. 'I'm sorry, but you're wasting your time.'

Carlo drew himself up to his full height, which was still some inches less than Mazzaro, she thought inconsequently.

'You disappoint me, Suzanne,' he said. 'I had thought that you would have got over your infatuation for the Conte by now!'

Suzanne's lips parted, and then she quickly closed them again. Steeling herself against letting him see how his words had affected her, she drew her chair jerkily up to the desk, and reached for the telephone directory. A white envelope was resting upon its open pages, and as her fingers closed over it, she realised the Turk had forgotten to take his tickets.

'I don't know what you're talking about,' she managed at last, relieved to hear that her voice sounded almost normal. 'Now, if you'll excuse me. . .'

Carlo stationed himself in front of her desk. 'I don't believe you, Suzanne. It might be interesting to tell Sophia of my suspicions. Mazzaro has always despised her for her—shall we say, emotional weaknesses? It would be reassuring for her to know that perhaps her husband is not as white as he would like to paint himself, *no*?'

Suzanne forced herself to look up at him. 'Are you threatening me, *signore*?' she inquired, with amazing coolness.

Carlo shrugged, and her nerve almost failed her. Even Abdul Fezik seemed insignificant beside Bottega. And then, as before, her door opened to admit the Turk.

'I regret the interruption,' he muttered, going straight to Suzanne's desk. 'The tickets. I forgot the tickets.'

'Oh, just a minute, Mr Fezik. . .' Suzanne got to her feet, still holding the envelope like a shield in front of her. 'Signor Bottega was just leaving. I—well, I'd like to speak to you, if you have the time.'

Abdul looked positively astounded. 'You want to speak to me?' he demanded.

Suzanne nodded her head, shifting her gaze to

Carlo, defying the angry menace in his eyes. 'I think that's all, *signore*, don't you?'

Carlo clenched his fists, but one look at Abdul Fezik's burly physique was enough to stifle any fleeting consideration of combat. Without another word, he left the room, and with a little moan of relief, Suzanne sank again into her chair.

Abdul Fezik studied her pale face for a moment, and then he held out his hand. 'The tickets, please, Miss Hunt.'

'What?' Suzanne's lids flickered up at him. 'Oh— the tickets. Yes. Yes, of course.' She handed him the envelope. 'Thank you.'

'You did not really wish to speak to me, did you?' he added, and then nodded as he saw her expression. 'I thought not. *Au revoir*, Miss Hunt.'

'Oh, please. . .' Suzanne couldn't let him go like that. 'I'm sorry. But—that—that man. . .' She shivered. 'I want to thank you.'

Abdul hesitated. 'You are nervous about him?'

'Only a little.'

But she was. Something else to torment her when she was alone.

'Is there anything I can do?'

He was unexpectedly sympathetic, and the aggression he usually displayed in her presence had disappeared to reveal an unusually gentle concern. It was almost the undoing of her, and tears were ridiculously near.

Summoning all her composure, she shook her head. 'I don't think so.'

Abdul inclined his head. 'Well, if you should change your mind. . .'

Her evenings stretched emptily ahead of her. Impulsively she stretched out a hand towards him. 'The—the concert. . .' she murmured. 'Could I change my mind?'

Abdul stared at her incredulously. 'You want to come?'

'If you still want to take me.'

'If I still want to take you?' Abdul gave a short laugh. 'Do you mean to tell me that you are actually accepting an invitation of mine?'

Suzanne looked doubtful. 'Yes. . .'

He shook his head. 'Women! How can a mere man understand them?'

She looked up at him anxiously. 'If you'd rather not. . .'

'Oh, no.' Abdul was very definite about that. 'But I am to understand the situation, yes? This is in the nature of a reward, is it not? Well. . .' he smiled, 'I am not one to kick a gift horse in the mouth, no?'

CHAPTER NINE

THE telephone was ringing as Suzanne dragged herself out of the depths of unconsciousness. She reached automatically for her alarm, pressing down the button, and then groaning as the shrill peal went on.

Thrusting back the bedclothes, she padded out of her bedroom into the living room, where the sound was more insistent. What time was it? she thought, blinking at the daylight filtering through the blinds. What day was it? Sunday? Yes—Sunday. She sighed.

'Hello?' She lifted the receiver and gave her number.

'Suzanne?'

A voice she had not expected to hear again made her seek the arm of the nearest chair for support. 'Mazzaro?' No thought now of formality.

'Suzanne?' His voice had dropped an octave. 'How are you?'

'I—I'm fine.' Suzanne pushed back her hair with an unsteady hand. 'Mazzaro, where—where are you?'

'In London.' He paused. 'I want to see you, Suzanne.'

'Oh!' She could hardly take it in. Was she possibly

still asleep and dreaming? Mazzaro—in London! She couldn't believe it.

'Do you not wish to see me?' he demanded, and there was a certain hardness in his tone now.

'I—I—' Ridiculously she hesitated. 'What time is it?'

'Time?' He was impatient. 'It is almost eleven o'clock.'

'Eleven!' Suzanne gasped. She had slept so late! Then she remembered—the night before, Abdul had taken her to the midnight premiere of a film in which one of his young cousins had a small role and it had been after four before she got to bed. It was the third time she had been out with Abdul in as many weeks, and she was no longer alarmed by his admiration. She had discovered the aggressive arrogance he displayed was nothing more than a mask to hide a basic insecurity, and beneath his blustering façade he was really a man of some sensitivity.

'Have I got you out of bed?' Mazzaro demanded abruptly. 'I'm sorry—I assumed you would be up by now.'

'I—I was rather late to bed,' she murmured uncomfortably, and there was a chilling silence. 'I—where are you staying?'

The silence stretched, and at length he said: 'Does it matter?'

'Of course it matters.' Afraid that he might ring off at any moment, she was reckless. 'Mazzaro, what are you doing here?'

'That is my affair, surely?' he retorted. 'Well? Do we meet or do we not?'

'Of course we *do*,' she mumbled miserably. 'Wh-when? Where?'

'My hotel is not far from where you are now,' said Mazzaro coolly. 'I suggest I pick you up outside your hotel in—say, an hour?'

'That would be fine.' Suzanne nodded, and then realising he couldn't see her, added: 'Mazzaro, I— I am looking forward to seeing you.'

'*Bene*. Until later, then,' and he rang off without giving her a chance to say anything more.

As Suzanne bathed and dressed, she tried not to speculate on Mazzaro's reasons for being in London. But it was difficult to think of anything else when at the prospect of seeing him in less than an hour, her pulses raced and her fingers were all thumbs.

Then there was the problem of deciding what to wear. She pulled out skirts and pants suits and discarded all of them. She eventually ran out of time and had to choose quickly, picking a midi-length dress of silk jersey, predominantly green in colour, but streaked with shades of yellow, blue and purple. She didn't like it once it was on, but she hadn't time to change again, and she tugged impatiently at the clinging, elbow-length sleeves. At least the neckline was low and round, and allowed what air there was to ventilate her overheated skin. Cork-soled sandals added a couple of inches to her height, and she grabbed a straw handbag and emerged from the area steps leading down to her basement apartment just as a long-bonneted Jaguar nosed against the kerb.

The car stopped and her breathing quickened when the door was pushed open and Mazzaro got out. In a cream denim suit and a matching shirt he was disturbingly familiar, and she held her bag with both hands to hide her agitation.

He came round to open the nearside door for her, and his limp was less pronounced than she remembered it to be. 'Suzanne,' he greeted her politely. 'Won't you get in?'

Suzanne looked into his face, that scarred face which she had found impossible to forget. What was there about this man that aroused these emotions inside her? Why, when Abdul made it increasingly plain that his intentions towards her were perfectly honourable, did she crave the attentions of a man who had made it equally plain that his were not?

She got into the bucket seat at the front of the Jaguar, and he slammed her door before walking round to get in beside her. He was parked in a restricted area, and Mazzaro concentrated on getting the car into the stream of traffic before speaking again. It gave Suzanne time to regain a little of her composure, to calm her nerves, and slow the erratic beating of her heart.

Now that she had more time to consider him, albeit as inconspicuously as possible, she could see a certain weariness about him, as if life was not going particularly well for him either. It aroused her anxieties, and inwardly she chided herself for such foolishness. Mazzaro di Falcone did not need her pity, or her. . .love. . .

Love! The word hit her like a physical blow. Was that what was wrong with her? Was that why no one else could reach her? Had she been searching all her

life for this man, only to discover now she had found
him that he was already married?

'I tried to reach you last evening,' he remarked at
last, as they emerged from the maze of side-streets
and one-way thoroughfares into Piccadilly. 'But you
were obviously not at home.'

Suzanne took a deep breath. 'No. I—I was out.'
It was inadequate, but what else could she say?

'With friends?'

Did he know where she had been? 'With *a* friend,
yes,' she nodded, wishing that last evening of all
evenings she had been available.

'I see.' His hands slid round the wheel. 'Did you
have a good time?'

Suzanne's nails dug into the plaited braiding of
her bag. 'Why are you asking me all these questions?'
she protested. 'You can't possibly be interested in
whether I enjoyed myself with—with someone else.'

'But I am.' He glanced sideways at her. 'Who was
it? Anyone I know?'

'Anyone—you—know?' She stared at him.
'How—how could it be?'

'Pietro?' He paused. 'Carlo?'

'Carlo?' Suzanne felt sick. 'Is—is Carlo in
London?'

'He may be, for all I know. He was a few weeks
ago, wasn't he?'

'Was he?'

The look he gave her renewed all her earlier apprehension. 'Don't you know?'

Suzanne's shoulders sagged. 'He—he told you?'

Mazzaro shook his head, and her eyes widened

uncomprehendingly. 'Elena told me he had been questioning her about where you worked in London,' he enlightened her flatly.

'Oh! Oh, I see.' Suzanne bent her head. But when he said nothing more, she looked up again. What was he waiting for? Why didn't he ask her if she had gone out with him? But Mazzaro's concentration seemed completely on his driving, and only the hardening of his jawline gave her any hint that he was not as indifferent as he appeared.

'He—he came to the hotel,' she volunteered at last, and when he still made no response, she blurted out tremulously: 'Well? Haven't you any more questions to ask me?'

Mazzaro shrugged. 'It doesn't surprise me.'

Suzanne sighed frustratedly. 'I didn't go out with him, you know.'

'Didn't you?'

'No!' glad at least in this instance she could be absolutely honest. 'I—I know what you said, but I didn't realise he was—well, making assignations with me!'

Mazzaro made an indifferent gesture, accelerating into the King's Road and following the signs for Richmond. He seemed to know London well, and Suzanne shrank back into her seat as the pressure of traffic took up all his attention.

Eventually, however, they gained the open spaces of Richmond Park, and finding an unoccupied area, Mazzaro pulled the Jaguar off the road and switched off the engine. It was incredibly peaceful considering its proximity to the metropolis, and apart from passing traffic the only sounds came from some children playing ball and a couple of barking dogs.

Mazzaro half turned in his seat to look at her, his arm along the back of hers. 'You look tired,' he commented ruthlessly.

Suzanne trembled. 'Well, thank you. I've just been longing for someone to say that to me!'

Mazzaro's eyes darkened. 'What do you expect me to say to you?'

'Oh, be honest, by all means!' Suzanne tried to be flippant, and failed, the tremor in her voice evident for anyone to hear. 'I could say the same about you.'

'I know it.' His eyes dropped to her mouth, to the unknowingly provocative glimpses of her tongue as she moistened her lips. 'I do not sleep well, Suzanne.'

'Don't you?' Concern obliterated her own pain. 'But I thought—you seemed to be walking so much more easily—'

'I am. My back is much improved. A friend of mine has been giving me some massage, and it is definitely easier.'

Suzanne frowned. 'A friend?'

'A doctor friend.'

Marina Rossi! It had to be. The name was indelibly printed on Suzanne's memory. Jealousy seared through her. To imagine this woman, whoever she was, touching him, massaging him. . . She felt almost ill at the thought of it.

Mazzaro was regarding her intently. 'What if I told you my—physical disabilities had nothing to do with my not sleeping?' he asked softly.

Suzanne's breathing faltered. 'Mazzaro—'

'This man you were out with last night, who is he? Do you care about him?' he demanded.

Suzanne's head moved vigorously from side to side. 'He—he's a guest at the hotel. I've only been out with him three times. But last night there was a midnight premiere of a film in which his cousin had a small part, and he invited me to go with him. If I'd known that you—'

She broke off abruptly. What was she doing? she asked herself irritably. Revealing her vulnerability to a man whose interest in her probably stemmed from something his daughter had said. He had made no effort to see her until now, when he had discovered that Carlo Bottega had been in London.

'Suzanne!' He was getting impatient. 'Go on! If you'd known what?'

She moved her shoulders in a casual gesture of dismissal. 'Well, if you had—warned me that you were coming to London, I could probably have—have postponed any engagement I had.'

It was not what she had been about to say, and he knew it. The mouth she had come to know so well twisted sardonically. 'I see.' He ran a lazy hand over the darkness of his hair, putting a strain on the buttons of his shirt so that one parted to reveal the cloud of fine dark hair beneath. 'Do you go out a lot?'

Did she go out a lot? Suzanne almost laughed, although it would have been an hysterical sound. Three times since she had come back from Italy six weeks ago. Because she preferred the melancholy of her own thoughts to the artificial gaiety to be found with other men.

Instead of answering him, she asked: 'Do you?'

Mazzaro's hand fell to rest on his thigh. 'What is that supposed to mean?'

'I should have thought it was perfectly obvious. I asked whether you went out a lot.'

His heavy lids hooded his eyes. 'Where would I go?'

'A man—a man in your position—you must be invited to lots of functions,' she exclaimed.

'Which I attend with my so-beautiful *contessa*, no?'

Suzanne's stomach muscles tensed. 'Per-perhaps.'

His balled fist evidenced his anger. 'You, of all people, should know that I take Sophia nowhere!'

'Why not? She's a beautiful woman. You've just said so.' Suzanne couldn't prevent the words from spilling from her lips. Her nerves were strung to such a pitch she was hardly aware of what she was saying. 'Why do you hate her so? If—if she was appalled at the time of your accident, is that any reason to go on punishing her? Fear of—of something like that is a perfectly human failing—'

'I know all about my wife's human failings,' retorted Mazzaro savagely, 'and my appearance has little to do with them!' His glance seared her. 'But forgive me, I did not know she had an advocate in you!'

Suzanne caught her breath on a sob, and thrusting open her door, she stumbled out of the car. Perhaps he thought she would merely stand outside until he invited her in again, whatever his feelings, he was not prepared for her to go running away across the common, her hair a honey-gold pennant in the stirring air.

With an oath, he swung open his own door and got out, his angry: 'Suzanne!' almost inaudible above the excited laughter of the playing children.

But she ignored him, rushing unsteadily on, panting in the heat of the June morning. Already the skirt of her dress was clinging to her bare legs, and the back of her neck was damp. Beyond the playing area was a clump of trees, and she paused in their shadow, fumbling for a tissue to wipe the area around her eyes and nose.

Obviously, he was more fit than even she had given him credit for. As she made to stuff the tissue back in her bag, his hand closed round her arm, just above the elbow, and he jerked her round to face him.

'What is all this about?' he demanded angrily, his lean face unusually flushed with exertion. He had dragged off his tie and unbuttoned the collar of his shirt, and from the swift rise and fall of his chest, she guessed he had been running.

'I—you shouldn't have come after me?'

'What was I supposed to do? Leave you to walk back to the hotel?'

'You might have done.'

'I may be unreasonable about some things, but abandoning a woman is not one of them.'

She sighed helplessly. 'Mazzaro, this is no good. . .'

'I agree.' His eyes darkened. 'Perhaps this is better—' And his hands fastened on her shoulders, jerking her towards him, his mouth finding hers with unerring instinct.

Her lips parted intuitively, and when his mouth touched hers she sank back against the trunk of the tree behind her, his weight pinning her there. Her legs felt weak, the hardness of his arousing a lassitude that made her slide her arms round his waist, hooking her thumbs into the belt of his pants, holding him closer.

'Is this better?' he asked huskily, his tongue exploring the tiny hollows and crevasses of her ear, and she trembled.

'People—people can see us,' she whispered.

He drew a little away from her, resting a hand on either side of her. 'And that bothers you?'

She wouldn't look up at him, half afraid to let him see the power he had over her. 'How—how long are you staying?'

'What, here?' he mocked, deliberately misunderstanding her. 'Or in England?'

'In England, of course.' She endeavoured to smooth her hair.

'That depends.' He straightened, releasing her. 'Come, I'll buy you lunch. We have to talk.'

Accompanying him back to the car, Suzanne tried to get a grip on herself. She had been kissed before. Kissing meant little—even kissing that devoured her and left her feeling weak and unsatisfied. . .

The boys who were playing football cheered when a ball came their way and Mazzaro kicked it back with such force that it passed the pile of sweaters forming the goal-mouth of the opposing side. He grinned sheepishly at Suzanne as they got into the car, and her heart turned over. She hardly knew Mazzaro in this mood, but like all his other moods, it was unfailingly attractive to her.

He took her to an hotel in Richmond where the tables were set out on a small balcony overlooking an ornamental pool. He ordered Martini cocktails, and spent some time studying the menu before deciding on the English roast beef and Yorkshire pudding. Suzanne said she would have the same, although in all honesty the last thing she needed right now was food. Then, when their chilled Martinis had been served, Mazzaro said: 'Did you mean what you said before—about Sophia? Or was that just intended to hurt me?'

Suzanne stroked the rim of her glas with her lips. 'Why would I want to hurt you?'

'I don't know. Revenge, perhaps?' he suggested quietly.

'Revenge!' Indignation made her eyes sparkle angrily. 'That implies an injury on my behalf.'

'Oh, come on, Suzanne.' His green eyes bored into hers. 'If we continue to fence with words, we're going to get nowhere! You know as well as I do that we can tear one another to pieces!'

Her colour came and went again. 'And did I— hurt you?'

'Dear God, Suzanne, don't you know?' He glanced impatiently round the busy restaurant, and then looked at her again. 'Do you want me to show you my wounds?'

She looked down into her glass. 'You—you wanted to talk to me. . .'

'Not here!' he stated definitely.

'After lunch, we—we could go to my apartment,' she volunteered softly.

'I'd like that.' He reached across the table, imprisoning one of her hands beneath his. 'I'd like to see where you live.'

Suzanne could hardly get her breath. 'How—how is Elena? I—I thought of writing to her after I got back, but I didn't think you would approve.'

He half smiled. 'I should probably have confiscated all your letters and kept them myself. Suzanne, you don't know how much I have wanted to see you again. These past weeks, they have almost driven me out of my mind!'

'And—and yet it took—Carlo coming to London to bring you to see me!'

He uttered an expletive. 'Is that what you think?'

'Isn't it so?'

'In God's name, no! Suzanne, I did not know where you were. You had not told me where you worked. Have you any idea how many hotels there are in London?'

'Pietro could have told you.'

'And do you think he would have done so if I had asked him?'

'He—perhaps.'

'Not without broadcasting the fact. Forgive me, Suzanne, but I could not do that to Elena. She has so little. . .'

'And—she told you?'

He nodded, releasing her hand as the waiter brought their iced consommé. 'She was anxious about you.' He paused. 'Somehow Carlo had discovered that she knew all about you. After she had talked with him, she came to me. She was worried about what she had told him. Not half so worried as me, believe me!'

'When—when did you decide to come to London?'

He shook his head. 'It was not so easy. Contrary to the opinion you hold of a man in my position, I am not so assured. I was not even certain that you would want to see me.' He sighed. 'And I had begun a course of massage which had to be continued.'

'With your doctor friend,' said Suzanne dryly, swallowing her bitterness.

'Yes.' Mazzaro frowned. 'Tell me, why do you use that tone when you speak of it? Do you not approve of massage?'

'Of course I do.' Suzanne put down her spoon abruptly and took a deep breath. 'All right, if we're being honest with one another, is your—your doctor friend female?'

'How did you know?' Mazzaro regarded her curiously.

Suzanne hunched her shoulders. 'One evening, when I was staying at Castelfalcone, you dined with some people called the Rossis, didn't you?'

'Yes.'

'Well, Pietro intimated—that is, his mother mentioned that someone called—Marina was home, and Pietro said that you and she had grown up together.'

'Is that all?' Mazzaro looked resigned. 'He didn't also happen to tell you that Marina and I were once expected to marry, did he?'

'As a matter of fact, he did.'

'Are you jealous, Suzanne?' He sounded astounded, but her expression gave him his answer. 'Why? Why? If I had wanted to marry Marina, I would have done so fifteen years ago.'

'Would you?'

He shifted exasperatedly. 'Yes. Yes. *Dio mio*, Suzanne, you have no need to be jealous of Marina, no need at all.'

'But she is the one who—who massages you, isn't she?'

'Yes. But that is over now. Besides,' his mouth twitched indulgently, 'there is nothing romantic about lying on a slab, being pummelled about by someone who is only intent on doing their job.'

Suzanne ventured to look at him. 'What is she like?'

'Who? Marina?' He shrugged. 'Small, and dark. Wiry, I suppose you might call her. She is a very nervous creature, and burns up all her surplus energy. You would like her, Suzanne. She is a good person.'

Suzanne moved her soup plate aside. 'Why didn't you marry her?'

Mazzaro sighed. 'I never regarded her in that light.'

'Did your parents want you to marry her?'

'Yes.' He too pushed his plate aside, and the waiter hastened forward to remove them. 'The Rossis were—*are*—a wealthy family. My father saw a way to recoup the family's finances.'

'And you rebelled?'

'It wasn't quite like that,' Mazzaro retorted dryly. 'Suzanne, if I had cared about Marina, nothing would have stopped me from marrying her. But I didn't— so my father and I had a series of rows which culminated in my going to work for an auction house in Rome.'

'Where you met Sophia?'

'Where I met Sophia,' he agreed.

The roast beef was served and Suzanne made a pretence of eating it. She was getting quite expert at this sort of thing, she thought wryly, and then found Mazzaro's eyes upon her and knew that he was not deceived. In fact, he appeared to eat little himself, and seemed as relieved as she was when at last the strawberry gateau was removed.

'Shall we have coffee at my place?' she suggested, tentatively, and Mazzaro immediately summoned the waiter for the check.

London simmered in the heat of one of those breathless afternoons when even the pavements seemed to reflect a brilliance that was dazzling. Those people who were about moved lethargically, as if drugged by the sun, and overhead the arc of blue sky was unrelenting.

Suzanne directed Mazzaro to the basement car park beneath the hotel, and then they walked out into the sunlight again to reach the area steps leading down to her apartment. In her haste to go out earlier, she had forgotten to open any windows, and the air inside the apartment was stifling.

Mazzaro closed the door, as she hurried across the living room to throw open the windows, and he surveyed the room with interest. Suzanne put down her bag and looked anxiously about her. Somehow everywhere seemed smaller and more shabby than it really was, and remembering the Villa Falcone, she wondered what Mazzaro must be thinking of this place.

'So this is where you live,' he commented quietly. 'It is charming.'

'Hardly that,' exclaimed Suzanne, picking up a cushion from the black vinyl couch and shaking it into shape impatiently. 'But at least it's mine.'

Mazzaro sighed and moved away from the door, taking the cushion from her unresisting fingers and dropping it back on to the couch. Then he cupped her face between his hands and looked down at her steadily.

'I like it,' he told her firmly, his thumbs caressing her cheeks. 'You have good taste.'

'It's cheap—' she began, but his thumbs moved to silence her lips.

'It is modern,' he insisted. 'Bright and functional. Exactly what an apartment should be.'

Suzanne breathed quickly. 'Stop pretending. It's hot and stuffy, and I didn't have time to vacuum this morning.'

His hands dropped to his sides. 'Shall we have that coffee, hmm? And do you mind if I take off my jacket?'

'Of course not.' Suzanne turned away, and walked quickly into the tiny kitchen. What a beginning! she thought miserably. Why on earth had she gone on about the apartment like that? What had she expected him to say?

As she set cups on a tray, Mazzaro came to the kitchen door. He had shed his jacket and unfastened his shirt almost to his waist, the sleeves rolled back to reveal the lean muscularity of his forearms. He propped himself against the door frame, watching her, and she had great difficulty in maintaining her composure.

'It's instant, I'm afraid,' she said, as the kettle switched itself off and she poured boiling water over the grains.

'So long as it is coffee,' he remarked dryly. 'Shall I carry that for you?'

'No. No, I can manage.'

She turned sideways to prevent him taking the tray, and her fingers slipped off the handle. The tray bounced down on to the formica surface again, splashing hot coffee over the back of her hand. She gasped with pain, letting go of the tray to rub her injured skin painfully, and Mazzaro stifled an oath and grasping her wrist dragged her towards the sink. The cold water from the tap took the heat out of the small burns, and within minutes she was all right again.

'Now, I will carry the tray,' he told her briefly, and went ahead of her into the living room, setting it down on the low table beside the couch.

Suzanne followed him slowly into the room. 'Thank you,' she mumbled awkwardly. 'I—I'm not usually so careless.'

Mazzaro's face was tense with suppressed emotion, and then he went abruptly towards her, taking her hands in his and raising the injured one to his lips.

'Suzanne,' he said huskily. 'Stop fighting me!'

She looked up at him nervously, knowing the dangers of the situation, but unable to remove them. In the overheated apartment, the masculine scent of his body was a powerful stimulant to her overcharged emotions, and all other considerations seemed to fade into insignificance beside the urgent demands within herself. His lips moved from her palm to her wrist, to the network of veins that quivered beneath his touch, the sensual caress of his tongue sending rivers of molten fire to melt her blood. Then his lips trailed the length of her arm to her shoulder, brushing the jersey silk aside to expose the smooth skin beneath.

As he moved closer, she felt the hard muscles of his legs brushing hers, and she inhaled the odour of the soap he used when her face touched his chest. Her lips moved of their own volition to caress his heated flesh, her mouth and nose filled with his fine hair.

'Suzanne,' he groaned, his hands sliding over her shoulders. 'Kiss me, Suzanne. Again! Hold me! *Dio*, Suzanne, who taught you to do that. . .'

'You did!' she breathed, winding her arms round his neck, and his mouth covered hers, imprisoning her lips with a hungry urgency that revealed his own need of her.

The ragged tenor of his breathing and the heavy throbbing of his heart deafened her ears to any other sound, and when the buttons of his shirt dug into her breasts, she tugged it aside to get closer to him. His finger sought the zip of her dress, and she felt the coolness of air against her back when his fingers spread against her spine. The dress fell in a pool of silk around her ankles, and he kicked it aside as he lifted her into his arms.

'Show me your bedroom,' he suggested softly, his voice hoarse with emotion, and she had no will or desire to resist.

'It—it's through there,' she murmured, burying her face against his scarred throat, gesturing towards her bedroom door, and he carried her towards it, pushing it open with his foot and closing it the same way.

He laid her on the bed and she looked away when his fingers went to the belt of his pants. Then he was beside her, his mouth possessing hers, and she didn't much care about anything any more.

The sudden knocking at the door of the apartment brought a groan of anguish from Mazzaro's lips. 'Ignore it,' he commanded her roughly. 'For God's sake, Suzanne, do not answer it!'

Suzanne lay for a few seconds longer. 'I—I must,' she protested. 'It might be someone from the hotel.'

Mazzaro rolled on to his back. 'Wouldn't they telephone?' he demanded.

Suzanne leant across to bestow a warm kiss on his cheek. 'I won't be long,' she promised, and sliding off the bed snatched up her silk robe and wrapped it closely about her. If anyone made any comment, she could always say she was taking a bath.

The first man who pushed past her into the apartment was a stranger to her, and her cry of fear was purely instinctive. But the man who followed him through the door was only too familiar, and as her eyes turned to him, she let out another gasp of dismay.

'Hello, Suzanne,' said Carlo Bottega sardonically, as his burly colleague burst into the bedroom behind her. 'A small world, is it not?'

'Wh-what are you doing here? How—how dare you break into my apartment uninvited! What is that man doing—'

'Save your breath, Suzanne!' Mazzaro appeared in the doorway to the bedroom, fastening the zip of his pants and buckling his belt. 'Our—intruders are here on business, are you not, gentlemen?' He spoke savagely. 'My dear wife has been up to her old tricks again, *no*?'

Suzanne put a hand to her head. 'I—don't— understand—'

Mazzaro slid his arms into the sleeves of his shirt. 'It is quite simple, Suzanne,' as the burly man who had entered the apartment first brushed past him. 'This—person—is a private detective, *no*? And we have just given Sophia grounds for a divorce!'

CHAPTER TEN

BUT we haven't—'

'Suzanne's protest died beneath the look Mazzaro cast in her direction. 'Do you think the finer points of our relationship matter to these men?' He shook his head. 'It is sufficient that we are here—and together, you know what I mean?'

'Of course she knows,' said Carlo unpleasantly. 'But I am glad you are taking it so well, Count. I was afraid you might—cause a little trouble.'

Mazzaro's resemblance to his Medici ancestors had never been more pronounced. 'This is Miss Hunt's apartment, Bottega,' he said quietly. 'And I am not foolish enough to attempt to fight both of you at once. If it offends your sense of pride that I make no effort to defend my marriage, I will endeavour to accommodate you at some other time.'

Carlo shifted sulkily. 'Don't threaten me, Count!'

'Was I doing that?' Mazzaro finished fastening the but tons of his shirt, and thrust it into the waistband of his pants. 'Are we to learn the purpose behind this visit?'

Suzanne envied him his calm. She herself was trembling violently, not least with the possibilities of what Sophia's divorcing Mazzaro might mean to her.

Carlo looked across at the other man. 'Pignatti!'

he said, gesturing, and the burly detective stepped forward.

'I am here on the instructions of the Contessa di Falcone, *signore*,' he announced in heavily accented English. 'With the information I can produce in a court of law—'

'*Bene, bene*!' Mazzaro silenced him with his words. He picked up his jacket and put it on, his eyes flickering broodingly over Suzanne's scantily-clad figure. 'So? Your work is done. You can go.'

'*Si, signore*.'

Pignatti moved towards the door and after a moment Carlo followed him. But he did not turn his back on Mazzaro, even though the other man made no move towards him.

When the door had closed behind them, Suzanne expelled her breath on a trembling sigh. 'Oh, Mazzaro. . .'

He nodded abruptly, raking back his hair with controlled violence, and beginning to pace restlessly about the room. His unease unsettled her, and with uncertainty, she murmured: 'Are you angry with me?'

'With you?' He stopped his pacing to stare at her, his eyes darkening with remembered emotion. 'Why should I be angry with you?' He uttered an angry expletive, 'Oh God, don't you know I love you?'

Suzanne swallowed convulsively. 'You love me?' She could hardly take it in, but when she would have gone to him, he shook his head.

'Let me think, Suzanne!'

She linked her fingers together. 'What—what will you do?'

Mazzaro dragged her gaze away from her, and his next words were chilling. 'Sophia is a bitch!' he ground out, through clenched teeth. 'I should have known better than to think she could change!'

'She—you—you have done this before?' Suzanne faltered, and he gave her an angry look.

'What kind of a man do you take me for?' he demanded. 'Dear God, Suzanne, I have just told you, I love you! I do not make a habit of making love to other women!'

'I'm sorry. But—when you said about Sophia being up to her old tricks again. . .' She shook her head expressively, and he uttered a grim acknowledgement.

'I am sorry, too, Suzanne,' he agreed harshly. 'You are bearing the brunt of the anger I have for Sophia.' He shook his head. 'We were going to talk today. Then you would have understood.'

'Understood, Mazzaro?'

He sighed and looked at her again, his eyes gentle once more. 'Put some clothes on, *cara*. Then I will tell you.' His eyes moved hungrily down the length of her body. 'I cannot go on looking at you without wanting you.' Then, as she turned away, he added: 'Love me, Suzanne. Whatever happens!'

She was reluctant to leave him, even for a moment, but he turned abruptly away, saying: 'Do as I say, Suzanne. Get dressed.'

With an unsteady breath, she went into the bedroom, emerging a few minutes later in slim-fitting jeans and a sleeveless vest. If anything the masculine attire was more revealing than her silken robe had been, and he indicated that she should be seated before he spoke.

'Where should I begin?' he demanded wearily, putting the width of the room between them so that he should not be tempted to touch her again, and she said quietly: 'Tell me why you married Sophia. Did you love her?'

He nodded. 'You are right. That is the place to begin—at the beginning.' He paused. 'Very well. I have told you about my father and about Marina. Can you understand my frame of mind when I first met Sophia? I was young, I was independent for the first time in my life, and she was very—*free*—with her favours.'

'You slept with her,' said Suzanne flatly.

'Yes.' Mazzaro rested one hand at the back of his neck. 'She was not the first woman I had known, but she was beautiful, and when she told me she was expecting a child, I had no reason to disbelieve her. I did the honourable thing, *no*? I married her. Only to discover that the only thing she was expecting was to be the new Contessa di Falcone!'

'But Elena. . .'

'Elena was born three years later.'

'But you—you loved her?'

Mazzaro's expression hardened. 'Perhaps. In the beginning. I admired her—and a man can do much for admiration.'

Suzanne coloured, and he went on: 'After my parents were dead and we came back to live at the villa, Sophia discovered that being a *contessa* need not mean a life full of incident and excitement. I was often busy, I had little time to entertain her. In my father's latter years, he had run himself into debt trying to maintain the Villa without an adequate income. I had to think of ways to get us out of debt, to make us—how do you say it?—solvent? Sophia was bored, so she sought—solace—elsewhere.'

'Did you know?'

'Did I know?' His jaw tightened. 'Of course I did not know. Although later I discovered there had been a series of tawdry affairs throughout the months we had been at Castelfalcone.'

'So—so how—'

'How did I find out?' Mazzaro heaved a sigh. 'I used to enjoy skiing. It was my only recreation at that time. We used to go to Cortina—you have heard of it? Cortina d'Ampezzo, the Queen of Resorts? It is in the Alps here, and the skiing is excellent. I used to spend days on the slopes, leaving in the mornings before Sophia was awake and coming back in the late afternoon to find her ensconced in the lounge with a circle of admirers.' He paused. 'One day I came back earlier than usual. I found her in our bed with a skiing instructor.' Self-derision tugged at his mouth. 'Ironic, is it not? Sophia seldom went out on the slopes!'

Suzanne's hands were clasped tightly together in her lap. 'Oh, Mazzaro. . .'

'I was shattered, as you can imagine. But even then I don't think my mind accepted it. I don't remember too well what happened. I went out of the

hotel and I took the cable up to the highest slopes.
I was in a disorientated state, not fit to attempt so
dangerous a descent. I remember beginning the run
and my skis going out of control. I suppose I must
have lost consciousness, because when I next opened
my eyes the man who had been with Sophia was
pouring raw spirit over me. It is strange when so
much else was forgotten, but I can remember that
quite clearly. I suppose the spirit must have briefly
revived me. I was in a terrible mess, I know. I think
Sophia's lover had come out after me because he
was afraid I might do something stupid, and Sophia
followed him. When they discovered how badly
injured I was, they must have panicked. No doubt
Sophia was afraid I would denounce her for what
she was if I recovered, and if I didn't, there might
be some awkward questions to answer about how a
normally proficient skier like myself should have
fallen. Whatever their motives, by making it appear
that I had been drinking, they covered themselves
and negated my real reasons for going out there.'

'They—they didn't leave you!'

'Oh, but they did. I had lost consciousness again,
and you have to remember how I must have looked to
them. Torn flesh, broken bones—I must have seemed
more dead than alive. Eventually another of the
instructors found me on a routine inspection of the
slopes.'

'But—but how could she leave you!' Suzanne
felt sick.

'You wouldn't, would you, Suzanne?' he mocked

gently, and she got up from her seat, unable to bear his cynicism.

'And now she thinks she can get what she wants by threatening to take Elena away from me!' he muttered.

Suzanne faltered. 'What do you mean?'

Mazzaro smote his balled fist against his thigh. 'You don't really understand what this is all about yet, do you, Suzanne?'

'Sophia—Sophia wants to divorce you—'

'Does she? Does she really?' Mazzaro's face twisted. 'Suzanne, Sophia could have had a divorce from me at any time!'

'Then—then what?'

Mazzaro stared at her for a long moment, and then he moved his shoulders in a defeated gesture. 'Suzanne, you're so—so—In spite of your independence, you're so—innocent, somehow. It's hard for me to explain the kind of woman Sophia is, but— oh, God! Suzanne, she wants *me*!'

'What?' Suzanne was pale.

'Crazy, isn't it?' Mazzaro raked desperate hands through his hair. 'But there are women like that, Suzanne. Women who get their kicks from having affairs with other men, while still imagining that they care about their husbands.'

'But she left you to die!'

'On the ski slopes—yes, I know. As I told you, she thought I was going to die. And just after the accident, when it was still touch and go, she became very—affectionate towards Pietro, because she imagined he was going to inherit the villa. But I began to get better, and she turned her attention back to me again. I was not interested. Any small remnant of emotion I had felt for Sophia died three years ago on the slopes above Cortina. But Sophia will not accept that. And like anything unattainable, it becomes that much more—desirable.'

Suzanne's legs almost gave way under her. 'Is— is that why you didn't want her to know—'

'—that I could walk? Yes, of course. There was always the chance that I might be able to convince her that—sexually, I was dead. Then she might ask for a divorce.' His mouth softened as he looked at Suzanne's deepening colour. 'And then I met you, and against my better judgement I allowed myself to become involved with you. Sophia must have guessed at once how things were. In spite of my efforts to appear indifferent to you.'

'The—the dinner party. . .' Suzanne breathed.

'Yes. When you looked so beautiful, I wanted to strangle Carlo every time he spoke to you.'

'But—but you could divorce Sophia!'

Mazzaro shook his head. 'I have Elena to consider. And Sophia is a very plausible woman. Could you imagine any judge giving custody of the child to me? Particularly if Sophia appealed to him—as a mother!'

'But she doesn't care about Elena!'

'She knows I do.'

'What about Carlo?'

'Carlo is just like all the other young men she has produced from time to time. She hopes to make me jealous. Don't you see?'

'And—and now?'

Mazzaro paced restlessly across to the windows, staring out broodingly. 'There have never been any other women, Suzanne. No one, until now. I never realised what an opportunity this gave her.'

'H-how?'

'Sophia is away right now. In Rome, visiting friends. She must have convinced Carlo to do this for her, bribed him in some way. And, poor fool that he is, he doesn't realise her intention.'

'But how did she know you were in London?'

Mazzaro paused. Then he nodded. 'Pietro must have told her. Since Easter, he has scarcely been away from the Villa.'

'But his work at college. . . And when we met, you asked me whether I had seen him.'

Mazzaro turned to face her. 'Just because I am not jealous of Sophia's admirers, it does not mean I am without those feelings,' he told her. 'Did I not just explain? Seeing you with Carlo almost ate me up, and when Elena told me he was coming to London to see you—' He broke off abruptly. 'No doubt your rejection of his advances added to his eagerness to help Sophia.'

'Oh, Mazzaro. . .' Suzanne twisted her hands together, and he left the windows to approach her.

'I must not touch you, Suzanne,' he muttered huskily. 'There are things I must do before we can be together again.'

'What things?' Her eyes were wide and troubled. 'Mazzaro, if you can't divorce Sophia, and she won't divorce you without taking Elena away from you, what can you do?'

One of his hands reached out to twine itself almost irresistibly in the silky curtain of her hair. 'During these past few hours I have realised that I cannot let you go, Suzanne,' he told her roughly. 'God forgive me, but when I am with you, I cannot even think of Elena!'

Suzanne trembled. 'But—but you must,' she said quietly.

'Must I?' His eyes darkened with emotion. 'I ask myself, is it arrogance that makes me believe that Elena would not be happy with her mother—'

'Mazzaro! You know it's no good!' The burning pressure of tears stung her eyes. 'We can't live for the present, you know that. We can't take our happiness at the expense of the child's. You know Sophia doesn't care about her—even I could see that. Maybe not now, but at some time in the future, you would come to hate me, and yourself, for abandoning her.'

'I could never hate you, Suzanne.' He sighed. 'But perhaps you are right.'

'You—you know I am.'

'So—you are sending me away?'

Suzanne couldn't stand any more. With a sob, she buried her face in her hands, and when his arms closed around her, she pressed her face against the fine material of his shirt and wept bitterly.

Mazzaro allowed her to cry for a while, and then he said softly: 'There is one chance. . .'

Suzanne lifted her head, sure she must look terrible

now with puffy eyelids and tear-streaked cheeks.
'What chance?'

Mazzaro frowned. 'The collection.'

'The collection!' Suzanne blinked. 'How do
you mean?'

'I cannot sell the Villa, Suzanne. That is entailed
to the eldest male heir. But the collection is mine.'

'So?'

'It's worth a small fortune, you know that. The
paintings alone are worth several hundred million
lire! If I offered Sophia the collection—'

'But you couldn't!' Suzanne was horrified.
'Mazzaro, it means too much to you.'

'Not as much as you do, *cara*.'

'I—you can't do it. It's your life!'

'Not any more, *amorissima*. Now *you* are my life!'
He shook his head impatiently. 'If only I thought
Sophia would agree!'

'You think she might not?'

'I don't know. I don't know.' Mazzaro stared down
at her passionately. 'I only know I have to try. I have
to find out.'

'And—and if she agrees. . .'

'Then I can get a divorce—and custody of my
daughter.'

'If only it were possible!' Suzanne dared not hope.

Mazzaro stroked her pale cheek with the back of
his hand. 'You and I—and Elena. Yes, we could
make a good life for ourselves.'

'And—and the collection?'

'What is the collection compared to the love I have
for you, *cara*? An inanimate group of objects! I never

realised until now how unimportant they could seem.
Perhaps I never loved Sophia after all. I would never
have given up the collection for her.'

'Poor Sophia,' said Suzanne softly. 'I don't envy
her now.'

'Did you ever?' Mazzaro seemed surprised.

'As your wife?' Suzanne reached up to touch his
cheek with her lips. 'Of course I envied her.'

He moved his shoulders in regret. 'You've had so
little time, Suzanne. Are you sure you want me?'

'I love you, Mazzaro,' she breathed, and her words
made him catch his breath and pull her closely
against him. His mouth sought hers, but when passion
flared between them, he put her determinedly away
from him.

'I have to go,' he said.

'Go?'

'Yes. There are arrangements to be made for my
departure. With luck, I might get on the morning
flight to Venice.'

'The morning flight?' Suzanne couldn't help the
repetition. 'Will you—I mean—will you let me
know what happens? One way—or another.'

Mazzaro looked at her steadily. 'Suzanne, one way
or another, we will be together—of that I am certain.
Elena is ten. In six years she will be old enough to
choose for herself.'

'But you can't leave her with Sophia,' said
Suzanne wistfully. 'You know that, Mazzaro, what-
ever you say. But—if you want me—I'll wait.
However long it takes.'

'If I want you?' Mazzaro's mirth was full of bitterness. 'Suzanne, you'd better keep telling me I can't leave Elena, because something inside me keeps telling me that three years is long enough to live in my kind of prison.'

CHAPTER ELEVEN

SUZANNE was just leaving her office when Abdul came strolling through the lobby with Malcolm Norton. He saw her at once, and excusing himself from the hotel manager, he came to join her.

'Where have you been hiding yourself?' he demanded, half jocularly. 'I tried to reach you yesterday morning, and then again this afternoon. I wanted to ask you what you really thought of the film. We didn't have much time to talk on Saturday night.'

Suzanne endeavoured to remember what it had been about. So much seemed to have happened since Saturday night, and her memories of the film had been blurred by subsequent events.

'Oh, I enjoyed it,' she assured him, recalling the basic outline of the plot. 'I thought its politics were a little dated, but that kind of super-spy image seems to appeal.'

'You really think so?' Abdul watched her closely.

'Well, I've seen a lot worse,' she conceded, with a slight smile.

Abdul nodded. 'And what have you been doing with yourself? Norton tells me you've been out with a party of tourists or something.'

'What? Oh, yes,' she nodded. 'That Japanese party. Their courier has gone sick, and Mr Norton asked me to accompany them to Hampton Court.

Unfortunately, only a couple of them speak any English.'

'What an ordeal!' Abdul was sympathetic. 'Let's hope their courier has improved by tomorrow.'

'Yes.'

Suzanne nodded, but truthfully she had not been sorry to be out of the hotel. And at least conversing through an interpreter had kept her on her toes. She had had little time to think about Mazzaro, to speculate about the outcome of his confrontation with Sophia. . .

'You have some plans for this evening?' Abdul was speaking again, and Suzanne looked at him blankly for a moment, still absorbed with the turmoil of her own thoughts.

'I beg your pardon?'

'This evening? You are going out?'

Suzanne gathered herself with difficulty. 'I—why, no. No.' Then, realising what he was about to say, she added: 'I—I'm rather tired, actually. I thought I'd have an early night.'

Abdul hesitated a moment, then he nodded. 'Yes. Yes, perhaps that would be best,' he agreed. 'You do look a little—wan, no? An early night might do you some good.'

'I thought so.' Suzanne could smile more freely now.

Abdul nodded. 'Until later, then.'

'Until later,' she answered, and went lightly down the steps and out of the hotel.

The apartment was stuffy, but the cooler air of evening would soon put that right. She opened windows, took a few deep breaths, and then went to raid her small larder.

She wasn't particularly hungry, but she had to eat, so she prepared herself a cheese omelette. Then she set herself a tray, adding a yoghurt and a glass of milk, and carried it through to the living room.

She watched television sporadically, dividing her attention between it and the crossword in the *Daily Telegraph*. But it was difficult to concentrate on anything when, given free rein, her thoughts rioted over the scene which might be taking place at this moment at Castelfalcone. What would Sophia say? Surely she would not refuse the opportunity to become a very rich woman! And yet given the same choice Suzanne knew, with a sinking heart, that she would never give Mazzaro up. And Sophia wanted him. Might not his request precipitate the kind of action on her part he most wanted to avoid? Poor Mazzaro! Poor Elena!

At nine o'clock, she had a bath and put on her nightgown, returning to the living room to drink a final cup of coffee before going to bed. The ten o'clock news was just beginning, and she stood for a moment listening to the headlines before switching off.

The news of the crash came first. It was not every day that a hundred and forty-seven people lost their lives, particularly not when over half the passengers had been British holidaymakers. The crash had taken place in the Dolomites the newscaster reported. North Italian Airlines Flight 407 to Venice. . .

Suzanne heard nothing after Venice. She was hardly aware of dropping her coffee cup until the hot liquid spilled over her toes, and she sprang back automatically to escape the pain. Making no attempt to mop up the spilt coffee, she stepped nearer the television again, staring intently at the screen.

The initial statement of information was over, however. Now horrifying pictures passed before her eyes, pictures taken from the air at the scene of the crash. Fortunately the film was black and white, but even so the tattered remnants of clothing and luggage bore silent witness to the presence of their owners.

Suzanne watched in mute disbelief as the reporter's voice described how the pilot of the aircraft must have miscalculated his position and brought the plane down in the Dolomites only twenty minutes before it was due to land at the airport.

Back in the studios again, there was more detailed description of the crash and finally a telephone number to ring for further information. Suzanne snatched up her pencil and jotted the number down on the side of the newspaper, sitting staring at it for several more minutes before switching off the set and moving to the telephone.

The line was engaged when she first rang, and she waited impatiently for it to be free. Then she was through, and a woman's sympathetic voice was asking her her name and address, and why she was ringing.

Suzanne explained that she just wanted to find out whether a friend had been on the plane, and although she sensed that it was not a usual inquiry, the woman agreed to find out. Seconds later she was back with the news that someone of that name had been on the plane, and Suzanne just had time to replace the receiver before she passed out.

It was terrible being so helpless. All through the long night that followed, between spasms of frenzied weeping, Suzanne wished there was something she could do, someone she could go to and pour out all the misery inside her.

But her mother would not understand, and there was no one else. Mazzaro was dead; the Dolomites, which had been responsible for so much of his suffering in the past, had claimed their victim at last, and there seemed no justice in so cruel a blow.

She heard on the morning news that relatives of the victims of the crash were being flown out to Italy at the airline's expense to identify bodies and attend a mass funeral which was being planned for those who did not wish to bring their dead home. Funerals were terrible affairs, and yet Suzanne wished she could attend, although Mazzaro would no doubt be buried at Castelfalcone with his ancestors.

She even thought of going to Castelfalcone, only the thought of seeing Sophia again did not bear thinking about. Besides, if Carlo had heard that the Conte had been killed, perhaps he would withhold his evidence about them, and she could not risk putting Elena's happiness in jeopardy when she could never be closer to Mazzaro than she had been two days ago.

She looked so ill that morning that Malcolm Norton took one look at her before ordering her home for the day.

'In God's name, Suzanne,' he protested

impatiently. 'What has happened? Don't tell me nothing, because I know differently.'

It was almost a relief to explain. 'Someone I knew—someone I knew was killed in that plane crash yesterday,' she told him chokingly.

'Oh, Suzanne!' His tone brought the ready tears to her eyes. 'Why didn't you let me know? If you'd rung and told me, you needn't have bothered coming in at all today.'

Suzanne shook her head. 'I—I thought I might feel better with—with people,' she confessed. 'But you're right, I don't feel so good.'

Norton came round her desk and put a reassuring hand on her shoulder. 'I gather it was someone you cared about,' he said softly. 'I'm sorry.'

Suzanne nodded, not trusting herself to speak, and he drew her unresistingly to her feet, picking up her handbag and putting it into her hands.

'You know what you're going to do?' he asked, and she shook her head. 'You're going to take a few days off. Yes—' as she began to protest, 'I mean it. Go down to Bristol, why don't you? See that mother of yours. I'm sure she'd love to have you.'

Suzanne shook her head. 'My parents are away, in Germany. They're on a Rhine cruise.'

Norton heaved a sigh. 'Is that so?'

'Mr Norton, you don't have to concern yourself about me—'

'But I do concern myself, Suzanne. Heavens, you're not fit to be left alone!'

'I'll be all right, honestly.'

Suzanne was touched by his kindness. All the

same, she doubted if she would have gone to Bristol if her mother had not been away. Explanations of the kind she would have had to make were impossible right at this time, although the idea of getting away from everyday things was appealing. Her apartment held too many memories of Mazzaro, and their sharpness might well tear her emotions to pieces.

'So what will you do?'

Norton was speaking again, and she turned to look at him, an idea forming in her mind. 'Did you mean what you said about taking a few days off?'

'Naturally I meant it.'

Suzanne nodded. 'Then I will. I—I'd like to get away from—from London. Perhaps a few days at the coast would be a good idea.'

'What coast?'

Suzanne shrugged. 'I don't know. Sussex! Dorset! When I was young, we used to go to a place near Weymouth. That was nice, I might go there.'

Norton studied her pale cheeks. 'You're not thinking of driving there?' he asked anxiously, and she forced a faint smile.

'I'm not an invalid, Mr Norton.'

'No. But you are in a state of shock, Suzanne.'

'But it's not far.' The idea grew more attractive by the minute. 'If I left after lunch, I could be there by dinner time.'

'And what is this place called? I ought to know.'

'Westhampton Regis. It's a village. Just a few cottages, as I remember, and a shop or two.'

'Where will you be staying?'

'I don't know.' Suzanne made a helpless gesture.

'I expect there's an inn or a hotel, of some sort. You don't notice pubs when you're only eight years old.'

Norton looked doubtful. 'Why don't I ask Fezik if he'll drive you down—'

'No!' Suzanne was very definite about that. 'I mean—I'd rather you didn't tell him where I was going.'

Norton frowned. 'But I thought you had got to like him. You've been out with him, haven't you?'

'Yes.' Suzanne shifted uncomfortably. 'It's nothing personal, Mr Norton. I—I just need to be on my own for a while.'

Norton hesitated and she thought he was going to argue, but then he gave a resigned shake of his head. 'All right, Suzanne. I can't tell you what to do. But take care.'

It was some time since Suzanne's Mini had been out of the garage. Out and about in London, she invariably used the buses or on occasion took a cab, and she quite enjoyed being behind the wheel again. If only it didn't remind her that the last time she had driven she had been with Mazzaro. . .

She reached the outskirts of Westhampton Regis soon after five o'clock. The roads had been reasonably clear mid-week, and the unaccustomed concentration had been good for her. But the village she remembered had enlarged considerably, with new houses flanking the old, a modern shopping centre, as well as several hotels which all appeared to be busy with holidaymakers. Young parents with children were already wending their way up the narrow streets from the beach, making for the hotels and guest-houses, ready for the evening meal.

Suzanne felt a twinge of dismay. Of course—it was the height of the season, or almost. What if all the hotels were full? Although she had enjoyed the drive down she was tired now after her sleepless night, and looking forward to a bath and then bed. She didn't feel like driving on, looking for somewhere to stay.

Choosing the smallest of the hotels, in a side street off the sea-front, she parked her car on the forecourt and entered the lobby. A harassed receptionist was busily answering the telephone, while a handful of excited children darted in and out of what appeared to be the television lounge. Putting a hand over the mouthpiece of the telephone, the receptionist said: 'Can I help you?'

Suzanne stepped forward. 'I was wondering whether you had any accommodation. . .'

'Single or double?'

'Single.'

The girl shook her head. 'I'm afraid not. All I have to offer is a family room. We're a family hotel really. We don't get asked much for single accommodation here. Have you tried the Strand?'

The Strand was the largest hotel Suzanne had noticed as she drove along the sea-front, and she had hoped to avoid its imposing portals. But she shook her head now and said no, she hadn't.

'Well, that's the only place where you're likely to find a room,' said the receptionist absently, her eyes following the progress of the game going on behind Suzanne. 'I'm sorry.'

Suzanne nodded, and went out into the late afternoon sunshine again. Ought she to try somewhere else, or was the girl right? Was the Strand the only hotel likely to cater for her needs?

She reversed the car out of the hotel gates, and then discovered it was a one-way street and she couldn't get back to the sea-front that way. Sighing, she drove on up the road to where a junction signified Town Centre or Sea-Front. Choosing the latter, she turned right on to another of the narrow streets which led down to the promenade and was immediately confronted by another hotel sign. It was of a mermaid sitting combing her hair, and a chord was struck in her memory. The Mermaid! That was where she and her parents had stayed all those years ago. Was it an omen? It was worth a try at any rate.

But the receptionist at the the Mermaid was equally apologetic. 'I'm afraid we only have a double room with bath,' she told Suzanne regretfully. 'And that's due to a cancellation.'

Suzanne hesitated, thinking of the Strand and of what staying there would mean. Dressing for dinner, or at least changing, lots of bored, sophisticated people looking for diversion, and the curious eyes which would be turned on a girl staying there alone.

'I'll take it,' she said impulsively. 'The double room, I mean.'

The receptionist raised her eyebrows. 'You realise I shall have to charge you for the double room?'

'Oh, yes,' Suzanne nodded. 'I'll get my case from the car.'

The receptionist rang a bell on her desk. 'If you give the porter your keys, he'll get your luggage,' she said, pushing the register across to Suzanne. 'Will you sign this, please?'

The room overlooked the car park at the back of the hotel, but beyond the roofs of the buildings that sloped down towards the sea-front, Suzanne could just glimpse a line of deep blue. And the room itself was very comfortable, with modern furniture and fitted carpets, and a bathroom that she could move round in. A notice behind the wardrobe door indicated the times of meals and the routine fire arrangements, and as food did not appeal to her right now, she decided to have a bath and rest for a while.

She knew nothing more until the sound of early morning teacups rattling in the corridor outside her room awakened her, and she sighed with a deep sense of poignancy as the knowledge she most wanted to escape came irresistibly back to her.

The next few days passed in a kind of daze. She rose early in the mornings, had a light breakfast in the hotel, and then walked down to the beach. She remained there until lunchtime, drugging herself with the sound of her transistor, and allowing the sun to soak into her bones. After lunch, she would get into the Mini and drive, anywhere, it didn't much matter, just so long as she could get out and walk for a while until her feet and back were aching. Then back to the hotel in time for dinner, a couple of stiff drinks, and oblivion until the early hours of the next morning, and so on. If the other guests at the hotel thought she was proud and standoffish, she didn't notice. Besides, they were all people with families, and she had nothing in common with them. Nor ever would have, she thought in the depths of her despair. Now that Mazzaro was dead, there could never be anyone else. . .

The days passed remarkably quickly, and in no time at all it was the weekend again. She knew she ought to be considering returning to London, but Mr Norton had not said exactly how long she could stay away, and she dreaded returning to the empty apartment. She decided he could spare her another three days and tried to absorb the time that was left to her with a heightened awareness of its brevity.

On Monday afternoon, she returned to the hotel to find a sleek Mercedes parked on the forecourt. She immediately thought of Abdul, but it was not the same colour as his, and she breathed a sigh of relief as she entered the cool lobby.

A woman was standing by the reception desk, a small, dark woman, casually but expensively dressed, in maroon slacks and a cream shirt-blouse, the neckline slotted with a Jacquard scarf. She didn't look English, and as Suzanne crossed the floor to ask for her key, she heard her make an impatient comment in Italian. Immediately, Suzanne's nerves tightened, and the familiar ache behind her eyelids made itself felt. How ironic, she thought bitterly, that there should be an Italian family staying at this hotel! Perhaps she would leave tomorrow after all, and not stay on until Wednesday.

The receptionist looked up and saw her hovering behind the other woman. 'There you are, Miss Hunt!' she exclaimed with evident relief, as the Italian woman turned to stare appraisingly at her. 'This lady has been waiting for you.'

'For me?'

Suzanne's legs felt wobbly, but the Italian woman was looking at her closely and she endeavoured to appear calm.

'You are Suzanne?' the woman inquired, in accented English. 'Suzanne Hunt?'

'Well, yes, but—'

Brown fingers closed over her wrist. 'Come,' the woman said. 'We cannot talk here.' She cast an eloquent look towards the desk, but the receptionist assumed an indignant air. 'Can we go to your room?'

'Wait a minute. . .' Suzanne gently but firmly extricated herself from the woman's hold. 'Who are you? What are you doing here? Why do you want to speak to me?'

The woman halted and smiled faintly. 'Of course. I am sorry. My name is Marina Rossi—'

'*Marina Rossi*!' Suzanne's whole body went rigid.

'That's right. Mazzaro said you would recognise my name.'

Suzanne's composure began to crack. 'I—*signora*, that is—Signora Rossi, I don't know why you've come to see me, but—'

'Why, Mazzaro sent me, of course,' the Italian woman told her gently, and Suzanne began to tremble violently.

'Mazzaro—sent—you. . .'

'Yes.' Marina glanced round impatiently. 'We cannot talk here—'

'Wh-why?' Suzanne licked her dry lips. 'Why did—why do you think Mazzaro would want you to come here?'

Marina stared at her uncomprehendingly. 'You must know how Mazzaro feels about you!'

Suzanne had the horrible feeling that this was all some ghastly nightmare, and that at any moment Marina would sprout horns and a forked tail. Beads of perspiration came out on her forehead, and the palms of her hands were clammy with sweat.

Pushing back her hair nervously, she said: '*Signora*, I don't know what you want from me, but—but nothing can change—'

Marina's expression softened. 'My dear child, if avoiding Mazzaro means this much to you, he has obviously made a terrible mistake.'

Suzanne swayed. 'Wh-what are you talking about? A-avoiding Mazzoro? Mazz-Mazzaro's dead, you know he is! Why have you come here to torment me?'

Marina's lips parted incredulously. 'Mazzaro— dead?' she exclaimed, and then looked beyond Suzanne to someone who had just entered the hotel. 'Mazzaro! Mazzaro, I've found her! *Caro*, she really thought you were dead!'

Suzanne turned slowly, convinced now that she was dreaming this whole thing, but a tall dark man was there to catch her when she passed out for the second time in her life.

*   *   *

She opened her eyes to the darkened contours of her room, and then closed them again quickly. The remembrance of the dream she had been having was still there, and she was loath to let it go. It had been so *real*. She had actually felt Mazzaro's arms around her, and even the woman, Marina Rossi, had been exactly as he had described her. A choking sob rose in her throat as the agony of knowing that Mazzaro was dead seemed too great to be borne, and a shuddering attack of weeping swept over her, making her turn her face into the pillow.

'*Suzanne*!' Someone's weight seemed to be depressing the mattress beside her, and the voice inside her head seemed to be almost audible. 'Suzanne, stop it! Open your eyes! For God's sake, Suzanne, I am here! Not dead, *mia cara*, very much alive!'

Her eyes flickered open reluctantly, half afraid of what menacing presence might be there in the room with her. She had heard of extra-sensory powers, of spiritual domination and possession, and yet did such beings emit warmth and breathing such as she could feel there beside her?

A man was seated on the bed beside her, a dark man, wearing dark brown suede pants and a bronze silk shirt, open at the neck to reveal the strong brown column of his throat. The drawn curtains made his features shadowy, but as he moved his head to look down at her she could see the network of scars that marked his lean cheek.

She started violently, but his hands on her shoulders stilled her shaking body, his voice gentle and reassuring.

'Suzanne! Suzanne, it's me. Mazzaro! Don't run away from me again.'

'Mazz-Mazzaro!' Her tongue clung to the roof of her mouth. 'You—you're dead!'

'No, I'm not. Suzanne, I don't know what malevolent spirit would tell you such a lie, but I am here. Very much alive!'

'The—the plane crash—'

'It was tragic, was it not?' Mazzaro's brows descended.

'They told me you were on the plane.' Suzanne stared at him weakly. 'Mazzaro, I rang the information centre—'

He sighed deeply. 'A terrible mistake has been made, *cara*. But I am here—and I am no ghost, believe me!'

She stared at him for a moment longer, and then with a little cry she projected herself up from the bed and into his arms. It was unbelievable, feeling his arms like hard bands around the slender bones of her body, his warmth and nearness reacting on her with devastating effect. She pressed her face into the hollow of his shoulder and wept, her tears dampening the collar of his shirt.

Mazzaro let her cry for a few moments, and then he propelled her away from him again so that he could look into her pale face. Now she could see that there were hollows round his eyes, and deeper lines on his cheeks than even she remembered. But his features were so familiar to her she felt she could have traced their contours blindfold, and her hands lingered in the hair at the back of his neck, caressing the slightly rougher texture of his skin.

'Oh, Suzanne!' Mazzaro seemed content just to look at her, to drink his fill of her pale beauty. 'What agonies you have put me through!'

Suzanne's brows drew together. 'Put you through?' she echoed. 'But—but why?'

Mazzaro expelled his breath on a sigh. 'I have been trying to get in touch with you since last Monday afternoon, Suzanne.'

'Last Monday afternoon?' If anything she went slightly paler. 'You mean—you mean right after the—the crash?'

'That's right.'

Suzanne shook her head. 'But I didn't know—'

'I know that now.' His eyes darkened. 'Oh, yes, I know that now.'

Suzanne stared at him uncomprehendingly. 'Then—then why—'

'Why didn't I get through to you?' Mazzaro shook his head. 'Oh, Suzanne, if only I had!'

She gazed at him helplessly, but the desire for him to explain was being undermined by the taut curve of his mouth, and Mazzaro, watching the sensual play of expression across her face, felt his own senses stirring irresistibly. With a groan, he put one hand behind her head, propelling her mouth to his, and she wound her arms around his neck, arching her body against him. Her lips parted beneath the pressure of his, her hands sliding over his back beneath the fine material of his shirt.

Eventually, however, Mazzaro made a determined effort and tugged her arms from around his neck, drawing back when she would have sought his mouth again, holding her a prisoner in front of him. She struggled protestingly, but he shook his head.

'Suzanne,' he said unevenly, 'we have to talk.'

And suddenly she remembered he had not been alone when he came to find her, and her struggles ceased as an awful feeling of apprehension filled her again.

'Wh-what have we to talk about?' she faltered, and Mazzaro closed his eyes against the unconscious appeal in hers.

'Don't look at me like that, Suzanne!' he begged huskily, opening his eyes again. 'God help me, I don't want to talk, but I have to.'

Suzanne moved her head slowly up and down, gesturing her understanding. 'You—you've spoken to Sophia.'

Mazzaro's jaw tightened. 'No, Suzanne. No, I haven't.'

'You—you haven't?' She swallowed uncertainly. Then: 'You've—you've changed your mind about—about wanting a divorce?'

'No. He sighed. 'Suzanne—'

But she was trembling now, only able to see one explanation for his hesitation. 'It's that woman, isn't it? That woman who was with you? Marina Rossi. Where is she?' Her head turned quickly in all directions, as if expecting to find her hiding somewhere in the room. 'She's very attractive, isn't she? You didn't tell me that. What does she really mean to you? Has she warned you not to—'

'Suzanne! *Suzanne!*' His agonised cry interrupted her rapidly-becoming-hysterical outburst, and he jerked her to him, to press her face into his chest. 'Suzanne, there's no easy way of saying it—Sophia is dead! Do you understand? Dead! It was she, not I, who was killed in the plane crash!'

Her fists which had been struggling with him were suddenly stilled, and she lifted her head to stare at him. 'You—you mean—'

'I mean that whoever told you I was dead had made a terrible mistake over the names. It was Sophia who was flying back to Venice on Flight 407. Sophia—and Carlo.'

'Oh, no!' Suzanne gazed at him in horror. 'Oh, Mazzaro, I'm sorry! I'm so terribly sorry!'

Mazzaro smoothed his hands down her bare arms, as if to calm her, and his voice was steady as he explained what happened: 'As—as a matter of fact, I was originally booked on that flight. . .'

'Oh, God!' Suzanne pressed a hand to her mouth.

'. . .but then I decided that as Sophia was in Rome—or so I thought—it would be more sensible for me to go and see her there. I knew where she was staying, and I was—eager to speak to her.' His lips twisted ironically. 'Life is strange, is it not? If Sophia had not told me she was going to Rome, I should in all probability have been on that other flight. Although perhaps not.' He shrugged. 'If I had seen Sophia and Carlo together, I might well have looked for another plane. I do not think I could have stood to fly home with them.'

'So—so you flew to Rome?'

He nodded. 'I left London at nine o'clock that morning. The Venice flight left a couple of hours later. I heard what had happened on the car radio as I drove home.' He made an eloquent gesture. 'When Sophia wasn't at the address she had given me, I hired a car to drive back to Castelfalcone. Of course, when I reached home and discovered she wasn't there, I guessed she must have gone to London. I was mad. Then we got the news—'

Suzanne pressed his thigh reassuringly, and he covered her hand with his own. 'That was when I telephoned you. I wanted to tell you what had happened. I needed you, Suzanne. And I wanted you to know that I was safe.'

'Oh, Mazzaro!'

He sighed. 'I was told you weren't in the hotel. . .'

'I wasn't. I took a party of Japanese tourists to Hampton Court. Their courier had been taken ill.'

'Well.' He nodded. 'I telephoned the next day. It wasn't easy, as you can imagine. There was so much to do and arrange.' He shrugged. 'I was told you did not wish to speak to me.'

'What?'

'It's true.' He shook his head. 'I—I couldn't believe it.'

'Oh, darling. . .' Her hand sought his cheek, and he turned his lips into her palm.

'I telephoned several times during the next two or three days, and always the same answer. That was when Marina came into it.' He half smiled at her puzzled expression. 'Telephones are such unsatisfactory instruments. Somehow I had to get to you, to find out why you had changed—'

'But I hadn't!'

'I know that now. But I didn't then. Can you imagine my feelings? Sophia dead, and all the funeral arrangements to be made, and you—the one woman—' He broke off abruptly. 'Well, I had to know what had gone wrong, so I asked Marina if she would come to England in my stead to find you and speak to you, to tell you how much I loved you, and that if you no longer cared, life would mean absolutely nothing to me.'

His words made her lean forward and press warm lips to the curve of his jawline, and he shuddered with suppressed emotion.

'Let me finish,' he breathed hoarsely, and she nodded. 'So—' he ran unsteady fingers round the back of his neck, 'Marina came. And she saw your— the hotel manager, no?'

'Mr Norton?'

'Mr Norton, yes.' Mazzaro inclined his head. 'But he would not tell her where you were.'

'I had asked him not to tell anybody.'

'That was what he said. He said you had been taken ill and had gone away for a few days to recuperate. Unfortunately, he did not say why.' Mazzaro sighed. 'Still, Marina is a determined woman. She would not give up. She stayed on at the hotel, and in the bar on Saturday evening she encountered a friend of yours, Abdul Fezik.' He waited for her nod of recognition. 'This was the man you were out with the evening I was trying to reach you in London, no?'

'Yes.' Suzanne nodded.

'So.' Mazzaro hesitated. 'He was also responsible for the messages I had been receiving.'

'I don't understand. . .'

'How could you?' Mazzaro took a deep breath. 'This man, Fezik, had learned from your manager that you were ill and had gone away for a few days. Unfortunately, as with Marina, Norton did not give any reason for your illness, and—Fezik put his own conclusions to your behaviour.'

Suzanne shook her head. 'What conclusions?'

'He eventually told Marina that you had been frightened by some Italian who had come to the hotel to see you.'

'Carlo,' breathed Suzanne.

'*Si*, Carlo.' Mazzaro nodded. 'When my calls came through the switchboard, the operator being unable to reach you had asked this Fezik whether he knew where to reach you. When he learned that the caller was Italian, he put two and two together and made six, *no*?'

'Oh, God!'

'*Si*. That was when Marina telephoned me and told me that so far as she knew, you had not received any of my calls. When she also told me that you had been ill and had gone away—' He broke off, his mouth twisting with remembered agony. 'The funeral was over. There was nothing to keep me in Castel- falcone but common decency. And I regret to say that such proprieties fell far short of my need to know where you were and how you were. When I got to London. I went straight to your manager and—

how do you say?—laid my cards on the table? That was when I learned that you imagined I was dead! Oh, Suzanne, you have no idea of the torment you have caused me. I was so afraid you might have done something stupid. Norton told us you were in Westhampton Regis, but even he did not know where, and today we have visited every hotel asking for you.'

Suzanne expelled a trembling breath and drew closer to him. 'Oh, Mazzaro, I don't know what to say.'

'Say you love me!'

'I do, I do.' Her hands held his face almost reverently. 'I just can't take it all in!'

Mazzaro was solemn. 'You realise what Sophia's death means, don't you?' She nodded. 'And—after a decent interval has elapsed, you will marry me?'

'You know I will.' Suzanne's lips trembled. 'But what about—Elena?'

'Elena is fond of you already. You know that. She needs a mother—a *real* mother, not the casual affection of aunts and cousins!'

Suzanne quivered. 'Zia Tommasa won't approve.'

'You might be surprised.' Mazzaro smiled. 'Pietro is another matter. But they are not important. What is important is where we will live once we are married.'

Suzanne frowned. 'I thought—the Villa—'

'I shall understand if you do not wish to continue living there,' he told her gently.

'Oh, Mazzaro!' She wound her arms around his neck once more. 'Why? Because of Sophia? Darling, I'm not afraid of Sophia. Not now.'

Mazzaro's eyes were intent. 'Do you mean that?'

'You don't really want to leave the Villa, do you?'

He shook his head. 'It is my home. . .'

'Then it's mine, too. If you want me. . .'

Mazzaro buried his face in her hair, and she could feel that he was trembling now. 'I want you,' he assured her huskily. 'Never doubt that.' Then he endeavoured to speak more calmly. 'As for Pietro— he shall take his pick of the collection. I know the money he gets will not last long, but he has a genuine feel for antiques, and who knows, perhaps given the opportunity he will make something more of his life. Without Sophia's influence. . .' His voice trailed away to silence. 'Zia Tommasa, as you know, enjoys her work at the Villa. I have in mind a property in the village, not too far from the Villa, where she and a servant could be very comfortable together.'

'Do you think she will agree?'

'Of course.' He spoke with a little of his former arrogance, and she hid a smile. 'But there is one more thing. . .'

'Yes?'

'Yes.' Mazzaro's fingers were unbuttoning the neckline of her sweater as he spoke so that his lips could caress the warm skin beneath. 'I want you to come back to Italy with me.'

Suzanne's breast rose and fell. 'Wh-when?'

Mazzaro's lips sought the hollow between her breasts. 'Tomorrow—or the day after.'

'I—I—my work—'

He lifted his head, looking at her half appealingly. 'I have spoken to Norton. He understands that the air of Castelfalcone will be better for you at this time than staying in the city.'

'But, Mazzaro, we can't get married at once!'

'I know that. I understand that I must wait to make you legally mine. But—' his eyes darkened, 'do not ask me to leave you here, because that is something I cannot do.'

It was all too much. Suzanne made a confused gesture. 'You seem to have organised everything,' she murmured, unsteadily.

'Only if you will be happy,' he answered quietly. 'You know how I feel about you. Without you, I am nothing.' He shook his head. 'Well? Can you bear to spend the rest of your life at Castelfalcone?'

Suzanne's lips trembled. 'I can't imagine spending my life anywhere else,' she confessed.

MEDICAL ROMANCE™

Fast-paced medical drama

**Heart-warming,
tender romance**

Impossible to put down!

**Four new titles available
every month**

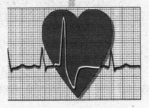

Available from

READER SERVICE

The best romantic fiction direct to your door